SHUT UP

SHUT UP

ANNE TIBBETS

OPEN ROAD
INTEGRATED MEDIA
NEW YORK

978-1-4976-6178-3

This edition published in 2014 by Open Road Integrated Media, Inc.
345 Hudson Street
New York, NY 10014
www.openroadmedia.com

For My Parents
Who did the best they could

SHUT UP

1

MARY

I creep out the front door of the house, closing it behind me as quietly as I can. Tip-toeing through the overgrown court-yard, I break into a run the moment I hit the sidewalk.

Faster!

Halfway down the block, new tears burn my cheeks and eyes but I don't care. I think about the rhythm of my foot-steps slapping on the cement, pumping my arms for speed. If I hurry, I can make it by sunset.

I whiz past the neighboring houses. An old man fusses with a lawn mower a few doors down. A teenage boy washes his shiny BMW on his driveway. When I see them I cross the street to the opposite side. This is no time for a chat.

I wish I'd taken my bike or skateboard, but it's too late, so I keep running. My lungs burn. Just as I slow to a fast walk at the end of the block, I see a car come to the stop sign at the corner, right smack dab in front of me.

Crappers!

I put my head down and wish that my awful short, bobbed brown hair hid my face. The car is a brand new Porsche station wagon. Dad calls those cars an "ego trip with wheels." There's a fancy mom driving it, and a bunch of soccer kids in the back seat. From the sidewalk, I can hear dance music screeching on the car stereo.

I wait for the car to pass, turning on my heel as casually as I can. I wipe the tears off my face. Showing my back to them, I pretend to inspect some roses on a nearby bush. I yank off my obnoxious thick round glasses and shove them into my back jeans pocket, with the thought that whoever's driving won't recognize me without them.

The roses are a total blur, but I keep pretending as I listen. The Porsche turns.

When I can't hear the car anymore, I plant my glasses back on my nose, and squint through the Coke bottle lenses as I watch the car disappear from sight.

Good.

The fewer witnesses, the better – especially by anyone who drives one of those. I rest my hands on the holes in my jeans for just a second before straightening up and breaking back into a jog.

A few steps into the intersection I hear a door creak open from behind. The widow who obsesses over her perfect rose garden is coming outside, probably to see if I breathed on her roses wrong. I speed up, pumping my arms again. The last thing I need is another lecture, of any kind.

When I reach the sidewalk on the other side of the street, I pinch my side to stop the stitch that's growing sharper. I want to look behind to see if the widow is watching, but think better of it.

Just then, I hear a bike coming toward me. My stomach drops. I'm afraid to look for fear it's Paul coming to talk me out of it.

"Whatcha' doin', Mary?"

It's not my brother; it's Ralph, the kid from next door. He has red bushy hair and a round belly. He's always been nice to me, so I look up at him and slow to a walk.

"I'm running away," I say, feeling my mouth go ugly with more tears. It feels good to tell the truth. I'm sick of lying all the time.

He raises his hairy eyebrows in surprise and stops peddling his bike, coasting for a while. His bike makes a flapping sound from a playing card he's clipped to the spokes on the back wheel. "Why?"

"Just because," I say. I'm not about to tell him any more. I've said too much all ready. Besides, the lump in my throat is so honking big I can hardly speak.

"Because why?"

"Just forget it." The rush I got from telling the truth is gone. He'll never understand anyways. I look at my sneakers and walk faster. I shove my hands deep into my pockets and play with some lint I find at the bottom. Now I wish he'd go away because I feel stupid.

Ralph has to peddle to keep up. "Is this about your sister?"

I freak. "Leave me alone!" A sob plops out as I run ahead. I can't control it now. I'm a blubbering mess.

I leave Ralph in the dust. My mind's swirling.

That stupid Ralph! Even he knows about her! Stupid, stupid Ralph! He's probably on his way to my house to squeal right now. What does he know? Nothing! This isn't about her! It's about me! I'm doing this because I want to! I'm *doing this*.

Me!

I should have figured something was up when Mom interrupted my skateboarding in order to have a family meeting.

In my head, I ran through the possible news flashes as I

propped my board against the side of the house and went inside.

Either Great Grandma Ida had died (which was no real surprise considering she was one hundred and one years old, no kidding), or Suzie, our ancient eighteen-year-old dog, had finally kicked the bucket.

But Mom and Dad looked really upset, and Suzie was asleep with her head in her food bowl like always, so I began to doubt it was either of those.

They brought us into Gwen's room, which was a bit of a shocker, because Gwen freaked like a cat in water if you ever went near her room. Then, Mom sat on the bed while Dad took a seat at the desk. I sat crisscross on the carpet, as did Rose and Paul.

"Gwen is getting married," Mom said. She didn't look at all happy. In fact, Mom was about to hurl right there on the faded chocolate brown shag carpet in Gwen's room.

Woah.

I glanced back and forth from Mom to Dad and decided not to say anything. They both looked so awful, and I didn't want to make it worse. I usually did whenever I opened my mouth and spoke.

Paul shook his head in disappointment. I totally agreed. I didn't think The Creep was a welcome addition to the family either.

"The wedding will be right after Christmas," Mom went on, "when Chris has some leave."

The Creep was a Marine just out of basic training. He'd only been back a few weeks, but was leaving for more out-of-state training soon. Paul still shook his head. It was currently the end of September.

"And there's something else you should know," Mom said.

Dad cleared his throat loudly, which made Mom stop. She pushed her glasses up her short nose. Dad's round face and bald head were purple, and his bright blue eyes were red and wet, like when he heard the choir sing 'Silent Night, Holy Night' on Christmas Eve, only now he looked like he'd just watched Suzie the dog get run over by a convoy of semis.

"Gwen is going to have a baby," Mom said.

Rose clapped her hands together, jumping up and down. "A baby? A baby!"

My stomach turned to ice.

Oh no.

This was worse than I thought. Not only was The Creep going to be a member of the family, but they were breeding more of them!

"Yes, Rose. A baby," Mom said, frowning. Rose squealed some more. Nobody else moved a muscle. Didn't Rose realize this was bad? Why didn't someone tell her this was bad?

Gwen was seventeen. I wasn't even sure if someone that

young was allowed to get married. To be fair, the whole idea of Gwen marrying The Creep wasn't really a shocker; after all, they'd been dating for two years. But what I didn't get was why Mom and Dad were letting her do it. They barely let me get the mail from the mailbox without a permission slip, and here Gwen was having a baby and getting married? It didn't sound right at all. I wanted to ask the question, but Mom and Dad looked so bent, I couldn't bring myself to say a word.

But wait.

How were they having a baby when they were forbidden from seeing each other? And, why were Mom and Dad letting Gwen do this when she'd been caught sneaking around to see him and lying about it? How was it that Gwen was getting what she wanted after everything she'd done to disobey Mom and Dad?

I opened my mouth to ask, but Mom cleared her throat.

"First, though," Mom continued, a catch in her voice, "there will be a wedding at church."

A wedding?

I nearly choked on my spit. Get out! Couldn't they just go to a judge or something? Didn't people do that? I mean, a wedding with a white dress and bridesmaids and The Creep wearing his dress blues Marine uniform, and a band? It was just too bizarre. A wedding was supposed to be a happy occasion, and the only one who looked like celebrating was Rose.

"Hurray! A baby!" Rose danced around in circles, clapping like a drunken circus clown. I wanted to lean over and smack her, but the squealing seven-year-old was out of reach.

Instead, I waited for Mom and Dad to yell at Rose, but they didn't. Mom just clamped her little lips together and ran her hand across the back of her neck, pushing her short dark brown hair back and forth. If I had said something out of turn like that they would have slapped me right across the face. No joke. But they didn't say a word to Rose. This bothered me almost as much as the news about Gwen.

"But we're not telling anyone about the wedding yet," Dad said, his lips flat and pale like a thick rubber band. "This is important. So don't say anything to anyone yet."

Huh? How come?

I waited for Paul or Rose to ask why, but Paul said nothing, and Rose just kept clapping about the stupid baby.

Mom and Dad might have said more, but by that point, I got lost in unasked questions. The family meeting ended, and that was that. Why was the wedding a secret? And where would Gwen, The Creep and the baby live? Instead of risking it, though, I left Gwen's room and walked down the hall to watch cartoons. I normally loved watching TV, but this time I just stared at it, only half looking at it.

A baby? A wedding? This was a disaster. Things like this weren't supposed to happen to people like us. I couldn't think of *ever* hearing about another family having this same problem, especially not in the stuck-up hoity-toity neighborhood where we rented this horrible old house.

Didn't Gwen know about birth control and all that? Even I knew from my health and development class – and I was only twelve!

I snapped the button on the remote and turned off the television. Everything was different now. And, although the thought of change wasn't all bad, worry stuck in my brain like a thorn. It didn't hurt a lot, but it was sure irritating. It was distracting. And no matter how hard I dug at the thorn, it wasn't coming out anytime soon.

2

MARY

My anger boils red hot. I swing my arms in the air as I run, punishing the air. I slow to a walk and try to calm down enough to catch my breath. It's too hard to run bawling like a big baby.

Stupid Ralph.

It takes me a second, but once I realize where I am, I panic.

Oh, rats.

I'm at Tammy's house. Tammy's been my best friend since the second grade, when we moved to California from Pennsylvania. Tammy's the only one who doesn't make fun of my hand-me-down clothes and my ridiculous glasses. I want to stop, but won't.

Tammy's brand new bike glistens on the driveway in the afternoon sun. If I'm not careful, Tammy will come outside, and within seconds I'll be invited inside for some of Tammy's mother's all natural oatmeal raisin cardboard cookies, and I'll end up losing my nerve. I can't have that.

I keep my face down and my hands buried deep into my pockets. I shuffle by the house as quickly and quietly as I can. Running will call attention, and walking slowly gives Tammy more of a chance to appear.

I strain to listen for the sound of Tammy's front screen door opening, or maybe her mom on the phone in the garage. Her mom always hides there when she wants to talk privately. But lucky for me, I hear nothing.

Once I pass Tammy's front yard, I sigh in relief. I jog down the hill toward the elementary school.

I used to like to skateboard alone in the side yard, which was this large cement slab with half brick walls on either side. It was quiet, out of sight from the inside of the house, and perfect for riding a skateboard back and forth a thousand times, and maybe doing a few tricks; or roller blading in circles, depending on your mood. I liked it there because it got me away from Rose, whom I was stuck sharing the same bedroom with. Rose was always following me around and wanting to play baby games, like dolls. Luckily for me, Rose didn't like to skateboard.

Paul did, though. Some days he would skateboard, too. I thought Paul was pretty cool, so that was always fun. Then one day, long before the baby, long before the pregnancy, and long before Gwen and The Creep were forbidden from seeing each other, The Creep strolled into the side yard as I was skateboarding.

He usually just hung all over Gwen. I couldn't think what made him want to come to the side yard. I didn't think he was there to skateboard. I saw him coming from the courtyard and quickly sat on the brick wall against the house, sliding the skateboard back and forth as casually as I could with one foot on the concrete. I didn't want to ride in front of him; if I fell, the teasing would have been endless.

"So," The Creep said, crossing his arms and leaning back on his heels. "What are you doing?"

"Skateboarding," I said, rolling my eyes at him. Dumb question – there was a skateboard right in front of me. *Duh!*

"All by yourself?" he asked.

"Yeah. Sometimes Paul or Ralph come out and do it, too." I thought maybe if he knew others could show up he'd take a hike. After staring at him for ten seconds in silence I realized he wasn't budging. *Drat.*

He grinned. "Is Ralph your boyfriend?" He looked like he was about to laugh.

I felt my stomach turn sour. He was making me feel weird again. He did that a lot. That's why I thought he was creepy. Just then, my foot slipped from the skateboard and it rolled away, banging against the wooden gate a few yards off. I stood up and got it, feeling The Creep's eyes on me. I sat back down quickly, with my back against the house, trying to act like it didn't bother me. He strolled over to stand in front of me again.

"No. Ralph isn't really my boyfriend," I said, watching him approach. I didn't want to tell him that Ralph had kissed me on the cheek just the week before in the bushes.

"Do you like him?"

I kept my eyes on the skateboard and started the back and forth rolling I was doing before, but it wasn't the same. It didn't feel right anymore.

"I think he kinda' likes me." I was sorry for saying that the second the words came out. I knew The Creep was having fun with me, but couldn't think how to make him go away.

The Creep smiled, proudly displaying his newly straightened teeth, but they still had the white scars from wearing braces too long. "Ralph likes you, eh?"

I nodded, looking back at the skateboard, but giving up

trying to slide it back and forth. He probably thought I was too ugly for a boy to like, just like Gwen did.

I could hear Gwen call me a fat cow and pushed it from my mind, answering, "Yeah." I rested my foot on the top of the skateboard.

"Do you like him?" he asked again.

"He's nice." I shrugged, blushing. I didn't want to talk with The Creep anymore. Well, ever, really. Why didn't he just leave me alone?

"Have you kissed him?"

I laughed too loudly and picked up the skateboard, setting it in my lap, as if adding it between him and me would help. "No!"

"Aw, come on! Pretty girl like you? With blue eyes like that? You've kissed a boy before!"

I felt my face turn hot. Now I was sure he was making fun of me. I knew beyond a shadow of a doubt I was far from pretty. Gwen reminded me daily. My teeth were crooked, my hair was a short mousey brown, and no one could even see my eyes behind my glasses. "I have not!"

"Sure you have! How old are you now, thirteen?"

I looked at The Creep and rolled my eyes, laughing too loudly again. "I'm twelve."

The Creep took a step forward and leaned in, as if inspecting my face. "No! Twelve? You look at least thirteen." I looked down at the skateboard and rubbed the top with my finger-tips, using my other hand to push my bra strap back under my tank top. I wanted to go back to practicing skateboarding but felt glued to the brick wall. I shifted slightly, feeling the pockets of my cut offs rub against the brick wall. I flipped the skateboard over in my lap and ran my fingers across the smooth British flag painted on the bottom.

"I'm only in the sixth grade."

The Creep moved closer. He stood right in front of me, his hands at his sides. I bit my thumbnail and looked up at him. He smiled. I wanted to back up but had no farther to go. "When I was in the sixth grade, I don't remember any of the girls looking like you," he said.

I felt my face flush and my stomach churn. The brick wall was like fly paper, with my rump stuck to it. I wanted to get out from in front of The Creep, but couldn't move. My breath quickened, and my heart pounded in my throat.

"Yeah, right," was all I managed to say.

"Those are nice shorts you're wearing," he said, eyeing my long legs up and down. His hand moved toward my knee just as Gwen appeared behind him, out of the front courtyard.

She stood at the end of the side yard and rested a hand on her hip. Gwen's big brown wavy hair and super long bangs were the exact opposite of her skin tight jeans and tee shirt. She was like an upside down carrot. "Mary?" Her eyes bore into The Creep's back. "What are you doing?" Gwen's usual nasty tone was not lost on me.

"Nothing!" I answered quickly.

To my relief, The Creep took a step back and crossed his arms again. "Mary has a boyfriend," he said, his voice instantly changing. He sounded just as irritated as Gwen.

"I do not!" I protested. The Creep cackled, head leaning back as he laughed. With long strides he walked to Gwen and slung his arm across her shoulders, turning her back to the front courtyard.

"Ralph, from next door. Though, I think she has a thing for me." The Creep led Gwen away.

"The little slut," Gwen said. Then they were gone, back into the house and out of my sight.

I felt hot tears swell in my eyes. I did not have a *thing* for The Creep! I hated him! He was a total jerk!

I sat on the brick wall, shaking. I wanted to punch The Creep. I wanted to slap Gwen. I wanted to scream!

Instead, I got up and flung the skateboard at the wooden gate. The faded avocado green paint chipped, and the wood dented as the skateboard skidded across the fence and slapped onto the concrete, landing upside down and rocking back and forth as it settled.

I saw the damage to the fence and burst into tears.

Great!

Now I'm going to get grounded for denting the fence when all I'd wanted to do in the first place was practice my skateboarding.

As the street flattens and turns a sharp corner toward the elementary school, my eyes catch sight of the front of a well-kept two story brick house. I stop walking, but only for a moment. The brick house was the first place we'd lived in when we moved to California. It was our dream home, Mom had said, at first. But then, Dad had lost his job, and soon thereafter, the house.

I scowl at the thought of where we live now, in that beat up old rental house. It smells musty and is embarrassingly outdated. Mom insisted that we kids shouldn't have to change schools when we moved, so we settled on the first rental we could find that fit our budget and was still within walking distance to the school. But, the rental, or "The Pit," as we call it, is a far cry from the old house, which was the American dream.

The American dream house was standing in front of me at the bottom of the hill; with its tree swing, back hill perfect for making forts, fruit trees and brand new carpet. The perfect house digs a hole into my pride and leaves a crater the size of Texas.

We're renters now.

We're renters in a neighborhood plagued with Mercedes owners, golf courses and mega-money. And here are us, tooling around in a twenty-year-old Chevy station wagon. Me, wearing Gwen's outdated hand-me-downs, and now, a member of the clan is pregnant at seventeen. We might as well wear tee shirts announcing ourselves as poor white trash.

I fight the urge to cry or throw rocks at the brick house. There it stands, the perfect home, ultimate perfection, and someone else's Mercedes is parked in the driveway.

After the side yard incident life was different for me. The Creep got even more Creepish. But only when others weren't looking. I just ignored him; I mean, after all, what could he do, really? I'd like to see him try!

Time went on, and Gwen and The Creep got more serious. They seemed to spend more and more time together. Mom and Dad didn't like for them to be alone, so they insisted Gwen bring him home after school so they could keep an eye on them. Unfortunately for me, that meant they were hanging out at home even more, with me, who wasn't allowed to go any where.

One day I was alone in the family room, watching TV after school. I'd stacked the chocolate brown pillows from the couch on the floor and sat on them, holding pretend reigns in one hand, and slapping the pillows with the other. I made clucking noises with my mouth to make the walking sounds. I sputtered with a neigh and rocked back and forth with the motion of the horse, lost in an imaginary world. It was peaceful.

Look, I realize this is babyish, but sometimes I liked to pretend I was someplace else. Besides, I loved horses. They're graceful, beautiful and elegant. Everything I wasn't. And we didn't have enough money for horseback riding lessons like Tammy, so this was as close as I was going to get.

Anyway, my horse and I were walking in a large green field with wild flowers covering the ground. Riding my horse was my favorite way of passing the time during commercial breaks between cartoons. Then Gwen and The Creep came in and I had a choice to make: I could keep riding my horse and let them see me, or I could stop and pretend like I wasn't doing anything strange.

I decided I liked to ride my horse, so I was going to keep riding, no matter what they said.

Big mistake.

The Creep and Gwen were whispering and giggling loudly, groping each other while sitting on the couch. They were so obnoxious they kept pulling me out of my daydream and away from the prairie. I flicked the reigns with my wrist and took the horse to a gallop, hopping up and down on the pillows as the horse ran faster.

The Creep suddenly burst out laughing and whispered in Gwen's ear again.

"Mary!" Gwen shouted, sounding irritated, as usual.

I didn't stop riding my horse, but slowed him back to a walk. "What."

"What are you doing?" Gwen never even talked to the dog this way, but I was used to it. The Creep was laughing so hard he was bent over.

"Riding my horse!" I explained. The commercials were almost over. I stopped the horse and swung my leg over the pillows to tie the reigns to a nearby tree branch.

"Well, knock it off," Gwen said. "You look like you're humping the pillow."

The Creep spit he was laughing so hard. "She's a natural!" Gwen smacked him in the shoulder, but he kept on laughing.

I didn't bother to say anything else. I took the pillows from the floor, stacked them on top of one another and leaned against them to watch the cartoon, crossing my arms and legs. The commercials were over now and the stallion would have to wait until Gwen and The Creep found someplace else to go.

I tried to concentrate on the television but couldn't

with Gwen and The Creep laughing like crazy behind me. The Creep had begun to tickle Gwen and now I couldn't hear a thing.

What did 'hump' mean, anyway?

My throat feels like sandpaper. I pass the elementary school and debate getting a drink, but I'm worried I'll lose my nerve, and totally chicken out. That's not an option.

Instead, I pick up the pace, trying to sprint. There's a group of kids I can see on the hand-ball and basketball courts. As I watch them, I feel totally alone, even more than usual. I wish I could play with them, but I don't know them and I'm not the best at meeting new friends. I've never had a lot of them; just Tammy and a few other girls who like to play in the Pretend Club that I started. None of them really knew me, though. I just play Pretend, making up elaborate fantastical stories, and I have the girls act out their parts. I would never tell them the truth about my life, or my family. I'm sure if they knew, I'd be an even bigger outcast than I already am. The only one who knows anything is Tammy. And even then, she only knows a tiny bit of it.

My eyes burn again with tears. The school offers no help. I tried once and it was humiliating.

If anything, school just proves what a loser I am. I run faster and try to think of something else.

3

PAUL

I cross the threshold of the front door and drop my swim bag in the corner of the foyer. Before I have the chance to dig out my wet towel, I hear them. They're at it again.

"I'll look the next time I'm at the store, Gwen, but it's too expensive," Mom says. She's using her high register voice, one decibel short of a shout. She puts her hands on her hips as she stands in the family room, notices me, but says nothing.

"Then if you can't get it for him, I'll pay for it myself, since this is just too much to ask!" Gwen yells.

"Oh, really? And how will you pay for it? You don't have a job!"

"I'd get a job if you'd just babysit!" Gwen throws her hands into the air like a drama queen.

"He's your child! He's your responsibility! You wanted a baby. Well, now you got one."

"Then, I'll just have Chris send me some money!"

"You do that, Gwen," Mom says, turning her back to Gwen. "We'll see how that works out."

Gwen mumbles something under her breath and flops her whiney ass onto the couch, crossing her arms and extending her lower lip in a babyish pout.

"Mary!" Mom shouts up the staircase from the landing below in the foyer. "You're supposed to be practicing!"

Leaving my towel, I skirt past Gwen toward the kitchen. She reeks of rage as she reaches across the coffee table to an overflowing laundry basket and sloppily folds clothes.

I rummage in the pantry for a snack and can only find an old bag of chips.

I snatch them and hide in the corner as I eat.

"Mary!" Mom shouts again. "Mary Elizabeth Green, you answer me!"

"She's probably up there picking her nose," Gwen says, folding the same tiny tee shirt over and over.

"Mary!" Mom bellows this time. She tromps up the stairs

with heavy and deliberate footsteps. "If I don't hear that violin in the next five seconds . . . !"

From the kitchen, I hear Mary and Rose's squeaky bedroom door open.

Mom's muffled voice can still be heard downstairs. "Rose, where's Mary?" she asks.

"I dunno," is Rose's response.

I tip the bag of stale chips upside down to drain the last of the crumbs from the bottom crevice. I hear a series of doors opening and slamming closed upstairs and take the opportunity to drink milk straight from the jug, being sure to keep out of Gwen's eye line so she has no ammunition against me. It occurs to me that Mary's probably in the side yard, and is going to get slapped to hell for not practicing. But this is nothing new, so I keep drinking the milk.

"Mary!" Mom hollers. A new tone creeps into her voice: panic.

Mom thunders down the stairs and turns the corner, passing Gwen in the family room to inspect the downstairs bedroom – which is Gwen's – the guest bath, and the garage.

When she re-enters the kitchen, her face is white. She doesn't even notice I hold the milk jug and not a glass.

"Have you seen Mary?" she asks. "No."

"The little . . ." She doesn't finish the sentence, pivots around, and her hands go to her head. "Paul, check the side yard."

I place the milk jug back into the refrigerator and slam the door closed. Without a word I go out the front door and cross that ludicrous courtyard to the side yard. It's empty.

Oh, man.

Mary's skateboard is abandoned in the corner. If she gets busted now, she's whipped for sure. Mom's already in a tizzy about Gwen. Once again, Mary has managed to make things worse for herself by calling attention. I know, and have tried to explain to Mary time and time again, the best way to live in this family is to be invisible. Mary can never seem to master that idea. And now with her pulling a disappearing act, she's sure to catch it.

I take a moment before I head back inside to tell Mom. I was kind of hoping a few minutes would calm her down, though I doubt it. There isn't much that calms Mom these days.

Gwen was a senior, and I was a freshmen. Before Gwen's car got taken away – after she snuck out to see The Creep one too many times – she would drive me to school every morning. We didn't talk. In fact, I tried to speak as little as possible to anyone.

Gwen drove to her friend Amy's house and picked her up, too. The two of them would gossip and gab the whole way to school, completely ignoring the fact that I was in the back seat. I didn't mind, honestly. I knew only half the people they were gossiping about, and the whole group of kids Gwen and Amy hung out with were immature idiots. One was always getting busted for drinking, smoking, or throwing a party at her house when her parents went on vacation. They never learned. They made the same mistakes, over and over. Yet, despite this, Amy and Gwen seemed completely entranced by the drama of it all.

One kid got grounded. One got hammered and smashed her brand new Jeep into a phone pole; a week later she drove to school in an identical brand new Jeep. One so-and-so got caught making out with another so-and-so, and one slut was having sex with a kid from the wrestling team.

I sat in the back seat and tried not to sigh in disgust too loudly.

Whatever.

I couldn't have cared less what Gwen did with her time, and the feeling was mutual. At least, I didn't care as long as they were gossiping about someone not in my own family circle.

Some days, Gwen would spend the entire car ride bagging on Mary to Amy. Half of the time she was razzing Mary for something that was completely normal for a twelve year old, like having tiny boobs, and long, gangly, hairy legs and un-plucked eyebrows.

It was the day I'd forgotten my Spanish homework in the back seat of Gwen's car that it had completely changed for me, when I suddenly cared about what she was saying. After school, I'd gone digging in Gwen's car and I'd found it, all crumpled up in the side door pocket.

It was a receipt from Planned Parenthood.

It took me a second to realize what it was. A "donation" in the amount of three hundred and fifty dollars, paid for with cash by Gwen Green. My hand shook and my mouth turned to cotton.

Gwen had had an abortion.

Nobody goes to Planned Parenthood and donates three hundred and fifty dollars for birth control!

I sat in the car, gripping the yellow crumpled paper for a minute, debating. It felt like an hour. I didn't know what to do.

I mean, Gwen was petty, cruel and obsessed with that asshole Chris, who Mary called The Creep; but if Gwen was having abortions she needed help. She needed to take the pill or something. Mom could help her with that, right?

I shoved the paper in my pocket and it stayed there for three days. I debated taking it to Gwen and came close once.

She was in her room with the door half open. I raised my hand to knock when I heard The Creep inside with her. Something made me stop; I moved in closer to hear.

"Would you stop it? Come on. . . ." Gwen's words were

strong but the little giggle she tittered immediately afterwards made her sound like she didn't mean it at all.

"Nobody's around," The Creep said. Sounds of kissing made me cringe. I raised my hand again to knock and then stopped a second time. What if The Creep didn't know about the abortion? As I debated, I waited, my hand held up to knock, yet frozen.

"My mom is home," Gwen whispered.

"So what?" There were more kissing noises and the rustling of sheets and clothes.

"So, she'll ground me again," Gwen said.

"That's never stopped us before."

"I know, but, come on, Chris. I said stop it."

There was a heavy sigh from The Creep and then his tone completely changed. "What's the matter with you? What's your problem?"

There was a pause from Gwen. Despite The Creep's nasty tone, which would have caused Gwen to scream and shout had it come from anyone else, I was surprised to hear her answer. "I just don't want to get pregnant again. I can't have another abortion. I can't. That's all. It really sucked, you know? I'll like, never forget that. And besides, I can't have sex while my mom is home. That's just gross." She sounded almost cautious, perhaps even afraid, so unlike the screaming banshee I knew her to be. "If we got caught . . . " she added.

"So what if we get caught?" I held my breath.

"My parents will kick me out," Gwen said.

"Big deal. You could come live at my house."

Gwen scoffed. "Yeah. Right."

"Why not? My dad doesn't care." I heard the bed squeak.

"Me? Live at your house, with your dad and brothers?"

What was wrong with Gwen? She's supposed to be so smart, and all. I couldn't understand how she didn't realize that Chris was totally manipulating her.

"Sure," The Creep said.

"No way. Maybe if we had our own place, but not with your brothers. That'd be just . . . weird."

"How would that be weird?" In the hall, I lowered my hand.

"I don't know. It just would," said Gwen.

"You're not, like, attracted to John, are you?" It sounded more like an accusation than a question.

"What? Oh my God. No way."

"Then what's the big deal?" The Creep pressed.

"I don't know. I guess I'm just not ready to move out, that's all."

"You want to be with me, don't you?"

"Of course," Gwen almost whispered. "And your parents hate me, right?"

Gwen gave an uncomfortable laugh. "Yes."

"Then you have to move out. Plain and simple."

"You just don't get it. In order to move in together, we'd have to, like, be married or something. My parents would never speak to me again if we were to shack up."

"Who cares if they never speak to us again? I mean, when have they ever done anything for you?"

Gwen gave no response to this.

"They treat Paul like some friggin' Golden Boy, ignoring you, not believing you about that whole mess with your ex-boyfriend in Pennsylvania. Right?"

This took me off guard. Matt Ferguson had been Gwen's boyfriend a few years back in Pennsylvania. He was way too touchy feely and I wasn't sure what happened exactly. All I knew was that when it ended, Gwen was never the same. She went from being a totally normal teenage girl to this raving lunatic who completely flew off the handle if you even looked at her funny. I had always figured it was the move that had messed with her head. Now, I wasn't so sure.

"Right," Gwen said, suddenly sounding like a kid.

"They're awful parents," The Creep said. "Seriously. The sooner you move out, the better off you'll be. And besides, it'd be so cool to have a place all to ourselves and not have to worry about your stupid little sister and getting caught and all that. Isn't that what you want? Isn't it?"

"Yes, but . . ."

"But what, Gwenie?" His temper turned fiery, he sounded oddly just like Gwen when she flew off the handle. "Don't you love me?"

"Yes, of course I do!" Gwen's voice was panicky.

"Then why don't you want to be with me? Are you breaking up with me?"

"No! I . . . "

"You're such a whore!"

Gwen gasped aloud. Outside the door, I put my palm up to open it, but curiosity and fear paralyzed my arm.

"I can't believe you would do that to me! I can't believe you killed our baby!" The Creep was yelling now.

I heard the rustling of Gwen's bed and knew they were both standing. I glanced around the hallway, looking for where I could make a quick escape. If The Creep discovered me, the consequences would be huge.

Gwen was crying now. "But, you said to have one. *You* said!"

"You make all these promises and then you don't follow through!" The Creep shouted. "What kind of girl are you anyways? You obviously don't love me as much as I love you. So you know what? Just forget it. It's over!"

I jumped across the hall and through the door leading to the garage. I could still hear them arguing in the hall.

"Chris, no! I love you!"

"Forget it. You're just a child."

"Chris, please!"

I heard the front door slam and Gwen's sobs. I waited ten seconds, then opened the garage door and stood in the hallway.

Gwen passed right by me, not looking up on her way back to her room.

"You okay?" I asked. I honestly felt bad for her. Gwen hissed at me like a cornered cat. "Drop dead!" So much for sympathy.

I watched Gwen as she threw herself into her room, slamming the door behind her.

She certainly made it hard to feel sorry for her.

Gwen stayed in her room sobbing for the rest of the day. That was, until The Creep called on the phone and they talked for an hour. I couldn't help myself and passed by her room, listening again. I could hear her apologizing and begging for forgiveness. It made me sick.

After that, I knew what to do with the receipt. But, somehow, in some way, despite the fact that Gwen was a horror to live with and that she was cruel to everybody but Rose (and vicious to her very core), I felt sorry for her. I mean, Mom and Dad were going to flip and totally forbid Gwen from seeing The Creep anymore, which would cause Gwen great pain. But, it was all for the better because Mary had been right, at least about one thing: that dude was a total Creep.

He was ruthless, blaming Gwen for the abortion when he was the one pushing her to have sex when Mom was home. Gwen was in way over her head.

I imagined her going to Planned Parenthood by herself, either with that loser she called a boyfriend, or with Amy, and stewing in the waiting area for her appointment. I imagined her having to wear a surgical gown and those terrible shower cap things on her head to hold her hair back, and crying because she was too stupid to use a condom.

And then my imagination turned, and I became furious at her. How could she sit in her car every morning and mock half the girls at school for being loose, and then allow herself to get knocked up by that Creep?

What an idiot!

She had nearly perfect grades. She was popular and got invited to all the right parties by all the right people. She wasn't stupid. Why was she making such terrible mistakes?

It's that Creep of a boyfriend! And to think, she had a baby with him! Oh my God, the baby! She killed her baby! That would have been my niece or nephew.

Think about that.

I felt a surge of bile gather in the back of my throat and I stuffed the receipt back into my pocket to fester for another day, and when I would carelessly dig it out again, the thought process would repeat.

Finally, I couldn't handle the weight of the receipt in my pocket any longer, and I found Mom in a calm moment, alone in her room, dusting. I showed it to her.

Mom's face turned to ashen white as she stared at it, disbelieving. I closed the bedroom door as Mom glared at the paper and nearly crumpled onto the bed as she sat, her eyes never leaving the faded yellow slip.

"I don't believe it," she said. "Where did you find this?"

"Her car," I said. I was sorry I'd shown it to her. She looked like she was about to pass out.

"In her car?"

I nodded. I left out the part about how I'd found it three days before.

"Did you show it to anybody else?"

"No."

Mom nodded then and, for the first time, looked at me, lowering the receipt. Her fingers had turned white with how tightly she gripped it.

"Okay, thank you," was all she said.

I waited for a second, wanting to comfort her, but also wanting to escape with every fiber of my being. Without another word, I bolted. I went straight to the garage, gathered up my bike and rode off, not even sure where I was going. The one thing I did know was that I didn't want to be around to hear Mom's sobs, or the shouting that would take place once Mom told Dad, or Gwen's screams when they spoke with her and forbade her from ever seeing The Creep again.

"I don't know where she is," Mom spit into the phone, the long stretched-out cord dragging on the avocado-colored linoleum. "I think she's taken off."

I sit at the kitchen table, my eyes following Mom as she paces back and forth across the kitchen. I hear Gwen make some snide comment from the family room, but choose to pretend I don't hear it.

"Can you think of where she would go?" Mom asks into the phone. She rests the heel of her hand against her forehead.

I brush my bangs from my eyes and watch. She's worried, but the expression quickly passes and fury replaces it.

"No, I already called Tammy's. They haven't seen her!" I stand. Mom reels on me like a tiger.

"Where do you think you're going?"

"To check the school," I say.

Her face softens, but only slightly. "Go." Then, back to the phone, "Yeah, you'd better come home. It'll be dark soon."

I breeze past Gwen on my way to the garage. She's still folding laundry. I do my best not to make eye contact with

*her. Though, I notice with disgust that she has a small sneer
etched across her lips.*

Bitch.

Since Mom and Dad had told us kids not to say anything
about the wedding, it was public knowledge less than a week
later, which was no big surprise to me. The very next Sunday,
we crawled into the station wagon after church and Gwen
started shouting.

"Rebecca knows about the wedding!"

Mom and Dad both turned all the way around from the
front seat. "What?"

"She knows all about it, and asked me about it after Bible
study!"

Both parents shouted the exact same question, overlapping one another. "How did she find out?"

Gwen turned her narrowed eyes onto Mary, who sat
between me and Gwen in the back seat. "Mary told her!"

"Mary!" Mom screamed.

Mary's eyes widened. "I did not!"

I watched Mary, and after feeling disappointed in her for
a few seconds, I realized that Mary was telling the truth. For
once.

Rebecca was a busy body youth advisor to the high school
group, and a loud-mouthed one at that. What really hap-

pened, I was sure, was that the advisor had found out from the minister's wife, who had been told by her husband, who had been told by Mom and Dad. But Rebecca didn't want to get the minister's wife in trouble, so she blabbed that it was Mary. Mary was prone to blurting things out that were none of anybody else's business, so she was the perfect patsy.

Either that, I figured, or Gwen had never asked Rebecca how she found out, or had told Rebecca herself, and when pressed by Mom and Dad, Gwen took yet another opportunity to throw Mary under the bus.

"I swear I didn't tell her," Mary cried.

Poor kid. She should just say she did and take the beating and be done with it.

"Don't you lie to me!" Mom shouted. The windows of the car could have shattered from the sheer volume of her scream.

"It wasn't me!" Mary insisted.

"What a mess," Mom seethed from the front passenger seat. "Can't keep your trap shut for anything, can you? You and your colossal big mouth!"

"I didn't even talk with Rebecca today," Mary added. I could tell Mary was beginning to panic, she squirmed closer to me, but having no evidence in her defense, I kept my mouth shut. Rose was in the far back seat in the rear of the car, craning her neck to get a better look.

"Honestly, Mary . . . " Dad said from the driver's seat. Mary was near tears now.

"She must have me confused with Rose, because I didn't even *see* Rebecca today," Mary offered, fighting to stay calm.

"We told you specifically, not to tell anyone about the wedding yet! Don't you remember? Weren't you paying attention?" Mom was half turned around in her seat, glaring at Mary with hot eyes.

"Not likely," Gwen said under her breath, though it was loud enough for everyone in the car to hear.

"And why would Rebecca lie about who told her?" Mom shouted.

"I don't know," Mary cried, her eyes overflowing with frustration. "But, it wasn't me."

"No TV for a week, Mary," Dad said, turning the car out of the church parking lot and onto the street.

"But . . . but . . . " Mary looked at me for reassurance, but all I could do was shake my head at her. I opened my eyes wide and gave her a look.

Don't say anything else. Just shut up!

"But, I didn't do it!" Mary shouted.

In a flash Mom's arm was over the front seat, slapping Mary square in the jaw with an open hand. Mary choked on a yelp.

"That's enough out of you!" Mom screamed, instantly silencing everyone in the car.

Mary gripped her face and held her breath to keep from sobbing.

Poor kid was trapped. If she said anything more she'd surely get a whipping when she got home, but if she didn't convince them of her innocence, Gwen would use this against her time and time again. Mary's eyes darted back and forth. She looked so confused. But eventually, I saw the defeat glaze across her eyes. Instead, she looked out across me to my window and bit her lower lip to stop it from quivering.

I tried to catch Mary's eye but she wouldn't look at me. Her expression went glassy. I could have sworn I saw a tiny piece of Mary's spirit floating out the window.

4

PAUL

The cat was out of the bag now. There wasn't any point in hiding it any longer. Mom and Dad and Gwen worked to book the church, pick the minister, hire the organist and soloist; Gwen got to buy a wedding dress from the JCPenney outlet store. The dress was an extra size bigger so Gwen could gain baby weight and they wouldn't have to pay for alterations.

Meanwhile, the volume and feel of the house took on an electric tone. Everything was about the wedding. Everything. It was insane. And as I thought would happen, Mary had the worst time adapting. She'd wait for a lull in the shouting to ask the dumbest questions of all. Like if she could have a ride to the library, or if she could go to Tammy's house for a while. Then she'd looked shocked and hurt when she was barked at and ridiculed.

"Not now!" Mom would snap, and Mary would recoil as if Mom had skidded across the floor in white fluffy socks and touched her with a shock.

I tried to warn Mary on several occasions not to bother Mom and Dad with stupid stuff, but Mary just didn't get it. Sure enough, she'd do it again and Mom would sigh heavily and look defeated, as if the very presence of Mary was a drain on her soul. "Not now," Mom would breathe. Then Mary would slink away, looking guilty.

Mom was on the brink of cracking at any moment, but Mary was clueless about that. Gwen's constant and relentless battling scraped all the layers of control from Mom. She was like a ticking time bomb.

If only Mary would stop talking and only listen, she'd be much better off. At fourteen, I'd figured out the less you speak, the less people notice you. I listened more than talked and this was an advantage. I watched more than participated in the family, and that was what kept me from sinking like the rest of them. Keeping quiet and hidden in the shadows was my peace. I explained this to Mary, but she didn't have control over her own mouth. I sat back and watched the rest of the family clustered in their misery, reacting off of Gwen's toxic fumes. It didn't affect me in the least. Hardly.

"We need a buffet at the reception!" Gwen shouted one day at dinner.

No one had been speaking at all – in fact, I had just been thinking how nice and quiet the meal had been. All that was heard was the clanking of forks and plates, and the setting of plastic cups back on the cheap wooden table. But Gwen wanted to remind everyone of the most important thing happening in all of our lives: her wedding.

"We can't expect people to come if they aren't getting food!" she added. She'd been asking for new things for the wedding daily, and Mom and Dad always said no. Yet, she kept asking. I had to give it to her; she was persistent.

Fact was, I knew Mom and Dad had borrowed the money to pay for the wedding from Mom's grandmother, Great Grandma Ida, who was in a nursing home. They were talking about it in the kitchen before they realized I was sitting there. They'd said it just wasn't right to spend someone else's money on a lavish shotgun wedding, and when they told Gwen, it sent her into another tirade.

Besides, Dad still hadn't found a new job and was working part time for his old company, and things were tighter than ever. Needless to say Gwen wasn't happy about this, and screamed continually. She wanted a wedding to be proud of, and it was plain nobody was proud. I mean, how could we be proud of a star student ruining her life?

I guess this was obvious to her and it cut Gwen deeply. And when Gwen was cut, she got yellish. When screaming at Mom and Dad didn't satisfy her anger anymore, Gwen found ways to get mad at Mary. It got so bad one day Gwen screamed at Mary for breathing too loudly. True story.

In spite of this, when Mary would come crying to me, I wouldn't comfort her or tell her I understood. She needed to wake up! I'd tell her to be quiet and not to get into it with Gwen. Mary, though, took this to mean to not fight back, but to stand there like a rug hung on a line as Gwen beat her with a broom. So, I think my advice only made things worse for her.

I knew part of the reason Gwen wanted a fancy wedding was because her friends had all abandoned her, and she wanted to show them up. It didn't make it any easier to like Gwen, but at least I understood why she was being such a bitch.

Gwen's "friends" had all stopped talking to her once they found out she was keeping the baby and getting married. Amy was getting a ride to school with someone else anyways, since Gwen had her car taken away, but Amy was also spreading rumors like crazy. Soon, instead of having lots of friends and talking about colleges, nobody would even look at Gwen. No one wanted to hear about the wedding, or be a bridesmaid even. They called her names to her face, like slut and whore, and talked about her like she wasn't standing right next to them, hearing everything they said. I saw it happen at school quite a few times, and told Mary to shut up around Gwen. I felt sorry for her. Even if she was a skank.

I ride my bike past Tammy's house and the school, but stop there to get a drink and shoot some hoops with a couple kids I run into. I figure if Mary needs a few hours to herself, let her have them. At this point, she's going to get whipped until next winter, so she might as well take advantage of it and stay out as long as she can. If I can help Mary by not finding her, that's what I'm going to do. I feel after everything I've done to her, I owe her that.

Right about the time it starts to get dark I get the feeling I should head back home and see if she's turned up. Though, I'm fairly certain Mary will get whipped enough to be sorry she ever came back.

When Mary was grounded from the TV for blabbing about the wedding, none of us kids could watch it. There was only one TV in the house, and it sat in the family room, dead center in the middle of everything.

I didn't even like watching TV; I much preferred going to the Recreation Center to play pool or swim some laps, or getting on my bike and riding around aimlessly, or hanging out at a friend's house. But for reasons of my own I was stuck at home, and now because of Mary, I couldn't even watch TV When I realized that Mom had hidden the remote and I was out of luck, I totally snapped. I stood at the bottom of the staircase and bellowed at Mary.

"Mary! Come here!"

Mary's violin stopped playing with an abrupt screech. She'd been playing the same song over and over and I had to admit it was adding to my mood; even if Mary was good at the violin, the repetition was eating at me. Play a different song!

Anyway, when Mary reached the bottom step I saw her look at me, all suspicious. Her normally soft eyes looked at me with confusion. It was so unlike me to be this loud.

I glared at Mary, gripping the rod iron railing with one hand while the other was clenched in a fist, dangling at my side. Mary gasped aloud as I grabbed her by the shirt with my loose hand and shook her back and forth.

"Do you even get that because you can't watch TV, that none of us can watch now? Don't you get it?" I was screaming.

What the hell was the matter with me? I was the one who

wasn't sinking. I was the one in control. And now, I'd lost it over the TV?

I couldn't stop myself.

"I'm sorry!" Mary pleaded. "Let go!"

"Not everything is about you, Mary!" My grasp remained tight.

"Paul! Let! Go!" Mary's face was turning purple.

The words came out before I could stop them. "You're so stupid! If you'd just shut up . . . !"

In a flash I felt a searing pain spread across my face as Mary's clenched fist punched me in the nose. Blood spurted out like a water balloon had burst. I instantly let Mary go and grasped my nose with both hands, trying to catch the blood before it stained the shag carpet on the stairs.

"*You* shut up!" Mary was screaming now. "I'm not stupid!" I'd never seen her that furious. She usually just slunk away and cried in her room when she got screamed at.

I swallowed the rocks in my throat and walked away, leaving Mary screaming on the stair.

"Don't you ever touch me again! Ever!" She hollered. "Don't tell me to shut up! I'm *not* stupid!"

Just by the foyer was the guest bathroom. I shot inside and closed the door behind me. I reached into the jar on the counter and stuffed my nostrils with cotton balls. I could still hear Mary screaming.

"You ripped my shirt! I'm gonna' tell Mom!"

I froze in place when I heard Mom's voice next. "What's going on here?"

"He ripped my shirt!" Mary yelled. "He got mad that he couldn't watch TV and ripped my shirt, so I punched him. Look at this," she said. "He ripped it!"

"You punched Paul?" Mom was mad again, her go-to emotion. "He ripped my shirt!"

I leaned into the door to hear Mom's answer and quietly reached down to push the door lock. I knew what would come. It would be the switch – offences that big were dealt with by the switch. It had been years since I'd been switched, but Mary seemed to get it every week. At first, it was a wooden spoon. But that had gotten broken. Then, it was a window scraper from when we used to live in Pennsylvania to chip the ice off the car windshield. But somehow again, that had gotten broken, too. Now, Mom used the handle of a fly swatter. If I was lucky, she'd use the plastic-handled one, and not the one with the wire handle; that would be like getting whipped with a wire hanger, and the thought made my veins turn to ice.

One whack for every year of your age. Fourteen whips.

No way.

I pressed my back against the door and firmly planted my feet on the floor. I'd live in the bathroom for the rest of my life before I'd allow that.

To my surprise, instead of a barrage of shrieking and a pounding on the other side of the bathroom door I heard Mom say to Mary, "Go change." And then, silence.

"But, but, it wasn't my fault." Mary was crying now. I heard no response from Mom.

"Mom?" Mary said.

Mom moved past the guest bath door and down the hall. "Mom?" Mary was crying. She quickly erupted into sobs. "It wasn't my fault! Mom! For once it wasn't my fault!" I heard weeping. I turned and pressed my forehead to the door feeling like the worst brother on the planet, but unable to bring myself to open the bathroom door.

"Mom?" Mary whimpered sheepishly. When no response came, Mary's footsteps scrambled up the stairs and her bedroom door slammed.

I turned around and slid my back down on the door, sitting with my legs bent and my arms resting on my knees. How was it that I'd done something wrong and Mary had to suffer for it?

I reached up and flipped off the light switch. Sitting in the darkness I could hear Mary screaming at Rose upstairs.

5

MARY

Past the school, down the hill, and through a development of houses, there's a park. My class stopped there once to eat a sack lunch after a field trip so I know where it is. It's on the way.

I'm thirsty, big time. The back of my throat scrapes every time I swallow, and I can't take it anymore.

Beside the blue rusted playground area, which sits on top of a giant sand box, there's an open field and a small baseball diamond. Some boys I don't recognize play a game, so I walk as casually as I can to the drinking fountain. After drinking a ton, I don't stick around but jog past the baseball field and cross the street to the boulevard that heads to the shops, restaurants and office buildings, away from the houses.

I feel safer now. I'm a good distance from home, more than half way. A plan grows in my head as I run. The sun is setting, and it will be dark soon. I know I'd better hurry if I'm to get it done by nightfall.

Suddenly, I feel hopeful. Freedom.

Soon, I'll be free. No more of them. Out of everything that will change, once my plan takes effect, the only thing I'll miss is Tammy. And maybe school.

I laugh aloud at the thought, jogging a little slower as I chuckle to myself. Never mind. Come to think of it, leaving school forever sounds like heaven.

School was hell. It had never been easy for me – that was true. I wasn't a brain, a jock, a popular girl, or one with any special talent. I'm the violin girl, the one lugging around a violin case all the time, the one who had to practice instead of playing capture the flag after school. Mom, who played the violin too, came to help the school orchestra during music class once a week, so I always felt the kids treated me differently after that, like I was a spy, or something.

Once everything erupted with Gwen, however, school got even worse for me. It was just too hard.

I didn't want to play the Pretend Club anymore. After a while the stress of keeping up with new story lines got to be tricky, with everything else swirling around my stupid brain. So, I just stopped. The other girls, aside from Tammy, found other things to do at recess and just like that, The Pretend Club was no more.

I also stopped writing. I used to like to write stories and pass them around to my classmates. I even wrote the stories with their names in it, and found that they liked them more when I did. But I didn't feel like writing anymore. I just wasn't in the mood. What if all of the sudden they didn't like them anymore? I just couldn't take that. So I stopped writing.

Eventually, the feeling infected my schoolwork, and then I didn't feel like doing that either. I stopped doing homework and played by myself on the bars at recess, ignoring Tammy. It seemed like everyone, not just my family, was picking on me, and I only wanted to be left alone. Alone, I was safe. Alone, it was quiet and there wasn't any yelling. Alone, there wasn't someone there pointing out every time I screwed up. I couldn't ever be wrong if I simply did nothing, alone.

But even that didn't work. I was wrong just by existing. One day, a boy, Jefferson Randall, offered me a free cookie at lunch. When I ate it, a group of boys burst out laughing and told me they had all taken turns spitting on it. It was proof that everybody hated me, just as I thought. I ran into the bathroom and washed off my tongue. I stayed there for the rest of lunch, sitting on the floor clutching my knees to my chest, talking to nobody, staring at the walls and listening to the noises of the other kids having fun and laughing out on the playground. It seemed so far away.

Another day, I played handball with a group of younger kids at recess but scraped my hand on the blacktop reaching for a low ball. When I walked across the playground to show the teacher on duty, I turned around and saw the line of younger kids behind me, making fun of the way I had been walking.

I was mortified. I tried to march away like it hadn't bothered me. But it really did. That day, I hid under the baseball bleachers.

Not only was I an idiot at home, but now the kids at school had all figured it out as well. I wished I could crawl into a hole like a rat and die. If only I could stop saying all the wrong things and doing all the wrong things. But, no matter how hard I tried, I couldn't do anything without screwing it up somehow. I ate, went to school, went to bed and did the same thing the next day, but I felt as if I was being followed around by a huge black rain cloud and everyplace else was sunny, and I knew it was somehow my fault for being stuck there.

My mood at school overflowed into home, and the one at home back-washed into school. Paul, my only ally at home, turned on me over the stupid TV, of all things. Feeling angry, I'd yell at Rose for stupid stuff, and then get into trouble for picking on her. It was a never-ending cycle of wrongness.

"Look at these shirts, Mary! Are you kidding me?"

I stood in the family room next to the ironing board and looked up at Mom in the space between my glasses and my face. The fuzzy peach blob was turning a bright shade of magenta.

"You call this ironing?"

My heart pulsed in my throat. I tried to swallow it down and searched for the right words. "I ironed them."

"You half-ass ironed them. They look awful!"

Mom threw the shirts back onto the ironing board and swung her hands to her hips. I tried not to move.

"I'm sorry," I said. I was so used to saying it, it didn't mean much anymore.

"Do them again! And this time, do it right!"

Mom stormed away, off to another part of the house to torment somebody else.

I breathed a heavy sigh and picked up the iron. I had

honestly tried to iron the shirts right. I'd even used spray starch I'd found in the cupboard over the washing machine. I picked up Dad's button down dress shirt and tried to see where I had made the mistake. It looked ironed to me.

The doorbell rang.

I laid the shirt down flat, buttons facing up, and smoothed out the sleeve.

The doorbell rang again.

For a moment, I wasn't sure if I should risk leaving the ironing in order to answer the door. Either way, I could get into more trouble.

There was a heavy knock from the front door.

I tilted the iron up on the board and went to answer it.

Paul was there with a police officer, and he looked like he was about to barf .

"Is your mother home?" the officer asked with a serious expression.

"Yeah, sure," I said, forgetting to let them in. Instead of running to find Mom, I turned around and shouted on the top of my lungs. "Mom!"

"What?" came the response from upstairs. "MOM!" I shouted again.

Mom appeared at the top of the stairs. "Quit shouting at me!

What is it?"

"It's Paul!" I shouted.

When Mom reached the door I could see the beginnings of another yell on the tip of her tongue, but the moment Mom saw the police officer standing with a very green Paul, all the air seemed to get knocked out of her, and she turned a faded shade of gray.

"Mrs. Green?" the officer asked.

"Yes?" Mom stood next to me and gripped the door with one hand.

The Officer stood there for a few seconds and then shifted his weight, the leather on his utility belt crunching, as he rested his hand on the handle of his flashlight which hung on the opposite hip from his gun. "There's been an incident. . . ." he began.

I looked at Paul's face. *Oh, crap!*

"Paul and two other boys were vandalizing vehicles."

"Vandalizing?" Mom gaped.

"Hitting oranges with baseball bats toward moving vehicles," the officer said. "One car was damaged. Luckily, nobody was hurt."

Mom's body tensed. "Mary, go finish the ironing."

Without a word I bolted from beside Mom and went back to the family room. The iron sat steaming on the board. Flustered and not sure what else to do, I set to work ironing the dress shirt. I could hear mumbling voices in the foyer, but

59

could not make out what words were spoken. No voices were raised. No shouting from Mom. Just soft murmurs and eventually, the front door closing and the rustling of bodies as Paul and Mom entered the family room and crossed to the kitchen.

"What in God's name were you thinking? What's the matter with you?"

Paul slumped into a chair at the kitchen table, looked down and said nothing.

"Have you no sense at all? You're lucky nobody got killed! If you'd hit a windshield of a moving car with one of those oranges, they could have crashed! Is that what you wanted to do?"

Without waiting for a response, Mom continued, "And this is the second time! Has being grounded all these weeks not meant anything to you? You finally get your freedom back and this is what you do? You look at me when I'm talking to you!"

Paul craned his eyes upwards.

"Just wait until your father hears about this. You are in big trouble, mister! I'm talking chores for so long your grandchildren will be finishing them for you!"

Paul looked quickly to me, then back to Mom, saying nothing.

"No more after school activities for you for a month. Do

you hear me? You come straight home! No Recreation Center, no bike rides. If I can't trust you to have any sense, then you will have no freedoms. None!"

Paul mumbled something I couldn't hear.

"You'd better be sorry! Now march your butt upstairs this minute, and I don't want to hear from you again until your father gets home. Do you understand me?"

He nodded. "Then move!"

Paul sulked from the kitchen and past me at the ironing board on his way to the stairs.

Mom left the kitchen after him and stood in the family room, listening to his footsteps pound up the staircase and for his door to close. When she heard it her eyes turned to me. I stood like a statue at the ironing board, the iron in one hand, the can of spray starch in the other. I was watching Mom, scared to death she'd start in on me. I was frozen in fear, when suddenly I realized the look on Mom's face.

Mom looked old. Her arms were hanging from her body like limp noodles, and beneath her glasses she had dark purple bags under her eyes. Her ears were ruby red and her jaw was tight and clenched. The moment she realized I was watching, her body language immediately changed, and her face, having looked defeated two seconds before, looked angry and flush.

"What are you doing?" Mom shouted.

I took a deep breath, bracing myself. "Ironing."

"Then get to it, Mary! And mind your own business!"

I dropped my face towards the cooled shirt on the ironing board and set to work. Mom left but I dared not look up. The only thought I had in my mind was, *Thank God Gwen's not home.*

A few seconds later I heard sounds of Mom's faint sobs coming from the guest bath in the foyer. I slung the dress shirt on its hanger, hung it on the laundry room door knob, and went upstairs to my room where Rose sat having a tea party with her dolls.

I climbed onto my bed and lay down. I felt sad for Mom. I'd never heard her cry before. Ever. She sounded a lot like a kid.

Then, to my surprise, my feelings changed and I felt angry at her. If she was so sad, why was she always shouting? And then, I felt guilty for causing Mom so much grief.

If only I knew what to do to make it all better.

But deep, deep down, I felt glad. Glad Mom was suffering just like the rest of us. Then I felt mad that she couldn't figure out how to fix it all, and then I felt guilty for feeling such terrible things about my own mother. I felt so many emotions at once, I wasn't sure how I felt.

Rose held up a tea cup and saucer. "One lump or two?"

I scooted off my bed and plopped onto the floor. "You've

got it set up all wrong. The spoons go on this side and the plates here."

Rose frowned. "Don't mess it up!"

"But you did it wrong!"

"Mom!" Rose got to her feet and scrambled out the bedroom door.

For a moment, I panicked; if I got into trouble right now, I'd get a whipping like no other, with Mom's mood.

Luckily for me, however, after a few minutes of searching, Rose returned to the room empty-handed. "Do you know where Mom is?"

I finished resetting the tea party. "No."

Life continued like that the next few weeks. In between screaming matches, plans were made for Gwen's wedding. But it was never a happy topic, and no one would bring it up on purpose. Then, it was Halloween. Not wishing to bother Mom by asking for something, I dug into the front hall closet and unearthed the retired Hobo costume both Paul and I had worn many times before. It was an old suit of Dad's with silly patterned patches sewn all over it. Also, there was an old hat with a hole in the top. That morning, I smeared soot from the fireplace on my face to make myself look dirty, and proudly showed Mom before marching off to school for the parade around the blacktop.

Mom cracked a smile. "Very apropos."

"What does that mean?"

"Look it up in the dictionary," Mom said, handing me my sack lunch and ushering me and Rose out the door.

"How do you spell app . . . app . . . What was it again?"

"Bye."

Later that night, I went trick or treating with Tammy, and filled an old and frayed pillowcase until it was almost too heavy to carry. While going from house to house, Tammy's mom kept bugging me, like she was waiting for me to change colors or something.

"So, Mary," Mrs. Reynolds said as we turned a corner and rounded the block, "How are things at home?"

I didn't look her in the face. I mean, besides being a little pushy, she was nice. I couldn't look her in the eyes and lie so I pretended to inspect the candy in my pillowcase. "Fine."

"You still taking violin lessons from your mother?" I watched my feet. "Yeah."

"You still enjoy that?"

No.

"Yeah," I said.

In fact, it was horrible. Mom would stand at the bottom of the stairs and shout up helpful suggestions to me while I practiced. I hated it so much, I fought practicing. It was this constant tug of war with me and Mom.

"And how are your brothers and sisters? Everybody well?"

I suspected she just wanted to know about Gwen and the wedding, but I wasn't about to volunteer any information on my least favorite topic. "They're fine."

Mrs. Reynolds blinked a few times and then narrowed her eyes. I could tell she wasn't buying it. "And your sister, Gwen. She's well?"

No, she's terrible. She's mean, and horrible, and is making my mom mean and horrible; and I don't know what to do about it.

I slowed my pace slightly as I fought to gain control over my mouth. It would have been so easy to tell her. I wanted to tell her. I wanted to tell her so badly! Maybe I could live with them? I could share a room with Tammy. And then I remembered Tammy thought the fact that I shared a room with Rose was one of the greatest injustices of all mankind, so I figured the answer would be 'no.'

Maybe I could tell her everything, and then Mrs. Reynolds could find me someplace else to live. But then, for some weird reason, I thought about Rose and Paul, and how I'd miss them, and the idea turned sour, and I pushed it from my mind.

"She's fine."

Mrs. Reynolds frowned, then catching herself, turned a fake smile to Tammy and changed the subject. "What have you two ladies been playing at recess lately?"

Tammy rolled her eyes at her mom and then shook her head. "Stuff."

I kept my head down, pretending to rummage through my pillowcase again. I had a feeling that Mrs. Reynolds knew everything that was happening at my house; she always seemed to know everything. Tammy and I had often heard Mrs. Reynolds on the phone in the garage talking about everybody in the neighborhood and speculating about what was happening behind closed doors. I was afraid of what would happen if the world knew the whole truth. Besides, I didn't want to think about that anymore. It made me sad.

And, it was a holiday, after all.

I reach the strip mall and dare not pause for a break. This is the home stretch, so to speak. I'm almost there. I can hear the freeway behind the shops.

I jog past the sporting goods store and the little Mexican restaurant Dad calls a "hole in the wall," I look into the windows of the diner, and my feelings of happiness vanish.

Every Sunday, without fail, after church, the whole family goes to that diner for brunch; now, that would be no more. Part of me was thrilled. No more listening to Gwen crab about the soggy French dip. No more Rose ordering a cup of croutons with dressing and calling it a salad. No more

Paul shooting frilly toothpicks into the ceiling with his straw. And no more of Mom and Dad griping every five seconds to straighten up, get your elbows off the table, quit slurping your drink, stop blowing bubbles, don't touch your sister, blah, blah, blah, blah.

I keep jogging but I feel a lump swelling in my throat, and I have to stop to keep from choking. I'm not going to cry. Not anymore. I'm done with them. Done! No more.

No more!

Anger brings the tingling to the inside of my nose, and my eyes blur with tears.

No more of anything. And this time, I mean it.

After Halloween, without fail, as it always did, came Thanksgiving. Thanksgiving was much more exciting than Halloween, but not in a good way. The Creep was due a few days leave from training before he was shipped someplace remote for more training, and he had promised Gwen he would come by the house. Or, at least, that was what Gwen said.

The few days that he was home, Gwen's craziness only got worse. She was a raving lunatic of bizarre moods. One moment she was sugary sweet, then the next she was a screaming maniac. It certainly didn't help that on Thanksgiving Day, The Creep never showed.

Gwen sat beside the phone, screaming at anyone who

came too close or was unfortunate enough to try and speak in the same room as her.

"Be quiet! Shhh!" Then she'd look at the phone like it was a puppy dog and then frown deeper than anyone the age of seventeen should.

It was finally evening when the phone rang. After having a short conversation with The Creep, Gwen informed Mom and Dad that he would not be home at all for Thanksgiving because his commanding officer at the base had it in for him, and that he had lost his leave and was stuck on base.

After Gwen ignored all Mom and Dad's questions, they gave up asking and Thanksgiving dinner was eaten. No one said much , though and the most that was spoken was something like, "Pass the gravy."

Later that night, I was in the upstairs bathroom brushing my teeth before bed. I overheard Mom and Dad talking in the hall.

"He probably lost the leave for insubordination," Mom whispered.

I stopped brushing so I could hear better, my brush dangling from my mouth.

"I wouldn't doubt it," Dad agreed.

"He shouldn't have promised her," Mom added.

Dad said, "We don't even know if he did. He could have

said, 'If I get leave I'll stop by,' and Gwen took it like it was solid. You never know with her. She hears what she wants to hear when it comes to him."

There was no response from Mom, so I spit out the paste that was dribbling out the side of my mouth and went back to brushing. Two strokes later I heard more voices and froze in place, bending my head towards the door.

"The boy's got so many issues with authority it's a wonder he's surviving at all," Dad was saying.

"I thought maybe they'd straighten him out," Mom said, sounding disappointed.

Dad only scoffed. "Once a punk, always a punk." Mom grunted her agreement.

"Something's not right. Gwen's not telling us everything, or he's not telling her everything," Dad said.

"I'll keep at her," Mom said.

There was a pause in the conversation, and having guessed I'd pressed my luck long enough, I started brushing again.

I don't know why, but a small part of me loved my parents just a little bit more after that.

A few days later, and with more grilling from Mom and Dad, Gwen finally told the truth. The Creep had lied. He had used his leave to go to Mexico to party with his friends on Thanksgiving Day.

After hearing this news, Mom and Dad fell into a silent shock and then got crazy angry. They went off! Not only was he a punk and a jerk, they yelled, but he was now a liar and an irresponsible child. If this was any indication of how he was going to behave after the baby was born, they said, Gwen was in for a terrible life.

But, Gwen, of course, would hear none of it. She shouted that Mom and Dad were only trying to control her by speaking badly of The Creep, and she was not about to fall for that. When Gwen was done screaming, she stormed off, leaving Mom and Dad looking numb. Mom said it would take a miracle, but she hoped Gwen would see The Creep for who he was, and cancel the wedding before it was too late. Dad shushed her and looked at me.

If it was even possible, Gwen became crankier after that. My guess was that Gwen was pissed off at The Creep but didn't want to admit it. It would only prove Mom and Dad right. Gathering enough strength one day, I asked Mom about Gwen's worse than normal attitude. Mom explained that it was because Gwen was feeling sick all the time with the baby, and because she couldn't go to her school Winter Formal with The Creep after he used his leave for Mexico.

But I didn't believe that for a moment.

You should have heard Mom go off on how ridiculous it was looking for a maternity formal dress, and a pregnant teen taking dance portraits and "boogie-ing" like a bouncing beach ball, but I tuned out most of it.

Something else was going on, I just knew it.

With the wedding day fast approaching and anticipation tight in the air, I spent most of my time playing alone in my room after school. Sometimes, Rose joined me. And, in an effort to avoid screaming, I let Rose play Barbies with me or even played baby dolls with her. It gave me something to do, and at least Rose didn't yell at me all the time. She loved to tattle, though.

6

MARY

Two mornings into Winter Break, I came into the kitchen to find Gwen sobbing at the table and Mom and Dad looking as grim as death. I slowed my steps. I considered coming back later, but the part of me who was tired of tip-toeing around Gwen and her problems was growing braver, so I walked straight into the kitchen and noisily poured myself a bowl of Cherrios. Besides, I was hungry.

And, come to think of it, Gwen cried all the time. How was this morning different from all the others? I honestly didn't care.

"This has to be a mistake," Gwen said, wiping her runny nose on a tattered tissue. She looked so defeated and puffy-eyed, I almost felt sorry for her. Almost.

I sat at the table and watched as Mom and Dad glared at Gwen. I poured a spoonful of sugar into my bowl, waiting for the inevitable scream for me to leave the room. When it didn't come, I took a bite of cereal and crunched away.

"What if it's not?" asked Dad.

"How can you even say that? Of course it's a mistake!" Gwen was back to yelling, causing any sympathy I may have felt to quickly evaporate – and there wasn't much to begin with.

"The police don't arrest people without cause, Gwen. We need to seriously consider canceling the wedding." Mom looked calmer than I had seen her in a long time, but her eyes were bright and darted back and forth between Gwen and Dad in quick, jerky moves.

Hmm. Who got arrested?

I crunched again.

Gwen's face turned bright scarlet. "Well! You'd just love that, wouldn't you?"

"Gwen . . . " started Dad.

"He didn't do this! Why can't you believe me?" Gwen stood up from her chair. The faded flannel nightgown she wore swayed as she swung her arms in the air dramatically;

her baby bump was barely visible. "That little Mexican twit is just lying for attention!"

"Gwen!" her mother shouted.

"You don't know that!" Dad's arms flailed as he spoke. "Mary! Go eat that someplace else!"

Oops.

I grabbed my bowl and sprang into the dining room. I plopped on the pleather chair and listened to the cushion hiss as I sank into the seat. Paul was already there, chewing his bowl of cereal, too. We looked at each other, then put our attention back to what was happening in the kitchen.

"She's lying! He would never do something like that! She got drunk while partying in Tijuana and had sex with his buddy, Richard, and now feels guilty and is accusing them all because she doesn't want to be a slut! It's so obvious!"

I heard the words but couldn't quite gather exactly what it meant.

Who? What girl?

I looked to Paul for a silent explanation, but he only shook his head.

"Why on earth would she do that? It's one thing to accuse one person of rape, Gwen. It's something else to accuse a group of boys who were all there together. If he didn't rape that girl, then he watched, which makes him just as guilty in the eyes of the law." Dad's voice was tight and terse.

"That's so unfair!" Gwen whined.

"Is it? How would you feel if it happened to you?" Mom added.

A gigantic sob erupted from Gwen's lips. "It *did* happen to me! Remember in Pennsylvania? Matthew Ferguson raped me and you never believed me!"

Holy crap! What?

Paul and I looked to one another. Matty Ferguson raped Gwen? I never knew that! Was that why we'd moved from Pennsylvania in such a hurry?

Mom sighed loudly. "The medical report said there were no signs of it being forced, Gwen."

Paul's eyes shot open.

Wait. She faked being raped?

I had so many questions I felt dizzy.

"How can you not believe me?" Gwen was hysterical now. "You never believe me! But now this happens, and you're willing to believe this? No! I know him. He would never do this!"

There was nothing but stiff silence as Gwen sniffed and sobbed. I looked to Paul again, he shrugged, but still looked like he'd seen a ghost.

"You need to see what's really happening here, Gwen," Mom said.

"No!" Gwen screamed. "This is my life! You can't tell me

what to do! You've already signed the consent form, I'm getting married, and then we can move far away from you! And you will never see your grandchild, ever!"

I heard Gwen leave in a huff, and then silence from the kitchen. Paul went back to his soggy Cherrios.

My brain was on fire. I dared not ask Mom and Dad to explain what was happening, and if I asked Paul just then, I'd get yelled at for sure. I had a million questions.

Did this mean that The Creep was going to jail?

How fantastic!

I slurped the last of my soppy Cherrios, relishing the thought. Things could go back to the way they were before, if he were gone. No more Gwen screaming all the time. No more of The Creep making me feel weird. No more of Mom and Dad on edge twenty-four hours a day. How great that would be!

Wow!

And that whole business about Gwen's old boyfriend Matty Ferguson in Pennsylvania? I vaguely remembered something about police coming to the house and Mom and Dad saying something about them telling Gwen she couldn't press charges against Matt. What was the term they used? Consensual? Whatever that means.

But it happened when I was eight, so my memory was foggy, at best.

For the first time in my life I heard Dad take the Lord's name in vain as he muttered and cussed under his breath.

". . . This is a nightmare . . ." he said, in between curse words.

I couldn't hear what Mom's answer was. I could only think one thing, over and over:

I always knew he was a creep.

Christmas came and went that year without fanfare. I could tell that no one felt like celebrating, except me. I held out hope that we would soon be free of The Creep.

He was going to jail! Yippee!

We went to church Christmas Eve, as we always did, and we got presents from Santa the following morning, but no one was particularly joyful. I played Santa, passing out each gift so they could unwrap them. Still, the air in the house tasted stale. Hoping to brighten the mood, I convinced Mom to play Christmas violin duets with me later in the day when we visited Great Grandma Ida in the nursing home, and Grandma Maggie and Grandpa Henry at their retirement condo. But even then the applause felt forced.

No one could escape the fact that this Christmas was three days away from Gwen's wedding to The Creep, and nobody wanted to rejoice. I, on the other hand, thought the entire problem was solved, and guessed they weren't as happy about The Creep going to jail as I was.

That night, though, everything changed. The Creep came over and announced that all charges against him and his buddies had been dropped. I felt my smile fade and my innards turn to rot. The Creep grinned from ear to ear as he announced that the girl in Mexico didn't have any proof. I noticed he did not deny it. Mom and Dad took the news with relief, but I could tell they were faking it. Gwen seized the opportunity to scream at Mom and Dad for ever having doubted him, and she and The Creep disappeared into her room for the rest of the night. In the past, that would have driven Mom and Dad insane; now, I think, they were just glad for the silence.

I, on the other hand, went up to my room and cried. Nothing was ever easy.

The day after Christmas, Rose and I were given matching powder-blue dresses Mom had found on sale at Target so we could light the candles at the wedding, and to my surprise, Mom and Dad wanted me to wear nylons to the wedding instead of those frilly little girl socks. They also let me buy some low-heeled pumps and get my ears pierced, even though I wasn't thirteen yet, which was the family rule.

On the way back from the mall, after getting my ears

pierced, I couldn't help but feel odd. Here we were, a day away from Gwen's "big day," (which no one was happy about), and I got to wear heels and get my ears pierced. I wanted to be excited and dance around like a lunatic, but couldn't bring myself to do it. I knew it wouldn't last. I would manage somehow to ruin the closeness I felt with Mom and Dad by opening my big mouth and saying the wrong thing. So, instead of speaking, I kept my mouth shut and sat in the back seat of the station wagon, smiling silently. It was all I could manage.

Then, the day of the wedding came. Everybody was running around the house like madmen. Mom was barking orders, the phone wouldn't stop ringing, and in the middle of it all, Grandma Maggie and Grandpa Henry had spent the night on the sofa bed and were in the way, slowing everyone down even more.

I was at the kitchen sink washing dishes after lunch. I wore my cut-offs and a zipped sweat shirt so as not to mess up my hair when I took it off. Mom had put my hair in large pink rollers. Before I even knew he was in the room, The Creep came over and gripped my hips with both his hands, one on each side, as he stood behind me. I tried to wriggle free but his hands were strong.

"Hey!" I shouted, moving to get away and squirting water all over the kitchen.

He pushed up against me for a second. I felt something hard against my backside.

"Get off!" I shouted, yanking with all my might and getting away, turning around to face him.

He smiled and moved in closer. I felt his breath on my cheek and wanted to barf.

"Ew, gross!" I yelled, turning my face away and pushing him back by the shoulders.

"What are you doing, Mary?" It was Gwen. Her hair was in even larger rollers and her make-up had just been plastered on. She looked a little ridiculous standing there in Dad's baggy blue sweats.

The Creep backed up and went and stood next to her.

"Look, Gwenie, Mary's getting hips," he said. "And her boobs have gotten bigger. She's gonna' be hot."

I felt sick to my stomach, literally. "You're a creep," I said. He just laughed.

I groped for a towel to dry my wet hands and left the room. As I ran upstairs I heard Gwen speak.

"Should I be worried?" she asked.

"Maybe I picked the wrong sister," The Creep said, and then started cackling that laugh of his again.

"You're sick," Gwen said.

"Oh, Gwenie. Stop making such a big deal. You're just hormonal and jealous because you're getting so fat."

On my way to my bedroom I passed Grandpa Henry on the stairs. He was dressed in his blue polyester suit and shiny white shoes and headed to the kitchen for a late lunch. He was a serious man and said little. From the look on my face, I guess, he stopped and watched as I went by. I looked at him with red furious eyes and opened my mouth to say something, but then I heard the sound of The Creep's laughter, quickly joined by Gwen's giggles, and I stopped.

My mouth closed and I turned away. Without a word spoken, I pushed my glasses up my fat nose and pounded up the stairs, disappearing into my room.

Once inside my room, I closed the door. Rose was playing baby dolls on the floor. It took a few minutes of sitting on my bed before I felt like looking at her.

"Mary, want to play with Rainbow Brite?" Rose asked, handing the doll to me.

"Leave me alone, Rose," I snapped, angry I couldn't lay down on my bed because of the stupid hair rollers, and just angry all around. I pushed back under the bunk bed as far as I could, hiding in the corner.

Rose's eyes filled with tears and her lower lip protruded. I popped. *She's crying over a stupid doll? She had no idea!*

"Stop crying, you big baby!"

Rose's face contorted into a red twisted mess as she bolted from the bedroom. When I heard Mom call for me, I knew I was going to get it by the way she had said my name. I slunk into the master bedroom where Mom had Grandma Maggie in a chair, her hair in rollers and half of her make-up finished.

"Did you call Rose a baby?" she was screaming so loudly she had a scratchy throat.

"No?"

I was not prepared for what came next. An open-handed slap crashed into my cheek. I felt my skin burn, and even though I didn't want to, I started to cry.

"That's for lying!" Mom said. "Go to your room and stay there until it's time to leave!"

I looked at Mom, holding my cheek in my hand. Grandma shifted in her chair.

"Honestly, Betty," Grandma said to Mom, "You must better control your children. In my day, a child who lied like that would be taken out to the shed and made to listen! That's how I raised you. And that's what's wrong with children today."

I turned to leave. I wanted to tell them, but there was no point in telling them about The Creep and the kitchen. They wouldn't believe me. No one wanted to hear me. I was in the way and a bother. I was a horrible sister to Rose, and pain in the butt to everybody else. What was the point of me even being alive?

Really.

Without saying anything, I slunk away and hid in the side yard until it was time to go to the church.

When the time came to leave, I was glad. Maybe then it would all be over. For the honeymoon, The Creep and Gwen were going away for five days. They were going to all the amusement parks: Disneyland, Knott's Berry Farm, Magic Mountain and Sea World. Mom and Dad said that it seemed silly, since Gwen couldn't go on any of the rides (because of the baby), but The Creep and Gwen said that was where they wanted to go. So once again, Mom and Dad gave up arguing. They were going to do what they were going to do, and they couldn't stop them.

When we arrived at church, Gwen's maid of honor was waiting for us in the parking lot. She had been in the school choir with Gwen. Her name was Heather. She had an old prom dress to wear for the ceremony draped over her arm, and her hair was pulled back in a French twist. The Creep's older brother, Josh, was the best man, and he was waiting inside the sanctuary.

The rest of the groom's family was waiting in the church as well, talking to Reverend McCormack, the youth minister who was to perform the ceremony. When we arrived, he shook Dad's hand and hugged Mom, and looked like he was as upset as they were.

When guests started to arrive, Gwen retreated into the Bridal Room where she was helped into her dress and Rose and I were escorted to the aisle so we could light the candles at the altar. Rose slipped a little on the black cobblestones steps, but for the most part, I was pleased with how we did. Then, Rose and I sat in the first row, waiting to watch the rest of the family walk down the aisle.

First, all the grandparents came: Grandma Maggie and Grandpa Henry, Mom's parents, and Grandma Dorothy, Dad's mom, who was staying at a hotel nearby. They walked with a hand on Paul's arm and held a little flower. I thought Paul looked good in his suit. Then The Creep, his brother and the minister, Reverend McCormack, came in the side door and stood at the front. The organ was playing some nice music. I knew the song but couldn't remember the name.

When it came time for Dad to walk Gwen down the aisle, everybody stood as the organ played, "Here Comes the Bride." Dad's face was purple. His ears were bright pink half-moon beacons on the sides of his head. When Dad lifted Gwen's hand to The Creep's, his hand shook. Things only got worse from there.

Reverend McCormack became emotional at seeing Dad so upset and started to cry, too. He choked and stammered through the whole ceremony; so badly, in fact, that even though I was in the front row, I had a hard time understanding what he was saying. He was speaking something about the seriousness of marriage and the lifelong commitment and such, and all I kept thinking about was how purple Dad looked, and how Reverend McCormack sounded like a frog. Mom looked white as a ghost, and each Grandparent would have been more excited at a funeral.

I glanced across the aisle at The Creep's family and thought they didn't look nearly as torn up. The Creep's mom, Deidre, was wearing a bright crimson red silk dress and sat next to The Creep's father, Ben, despite the fact they'd been divorced for years. The Creep's little brother, who had bright orange hair and a face full of freckles, wore a suit two inches too short for his tall basketball player frame and sat next to Ben, on the other side. They all stared straight ahead, listening to Reverend McCormack sob through the ceremony like there was nothing wrong at all.

Eventually, a singer took out a guitar and sang a song about marriage. It was the song Mom and Dad had had in their wedding, too. It was from a group called Peter, Paul and Mary. It had always been a family favorite. The trouble was, hearing it in Gwen's wedding poisoned the song for me. The singer was the choir director for my church's childrens choir. His name was Tom, and he had a thick mustache. He sang the song prettily enough, but I couldn't help frowning. I wished they'd picked a different song.

When the song was over, Reverend McCormack had The Creep and Gwen gave their vows, but he was still crying so it sounded like he was choking. Some of Gwen's high school friends had come to the wedding and sat there snickering and laughing the whole time. Someone shushed them, but that only made them giggle louder.

When Reverend McCormack announced them as husband and wife, the organist blasted the "Wedding March" on the pipe organ, and everyone in the church stood and clapped as Gwen and The Creep walked back up the aisle. Then we followed them up the aisle, as did The Creep's family.

After Gwen, The Creep and all the parents stood at the church door and shook hands, the family went back inside the sanctuary with the photographer and took pictures. I spent most of the time waiting in one of the pews. It seemed to take forever. By the time they were finished, it was past dinner.

When the wedding party arrived in the adjoining church fellowship hall where the reception took place, only a handful of people were still there, and the punch and nuts were completely gone. I told Dad that perhaps the guests left to get dinner when they saw there wasn't a buffet, and he frowned and said, "Maybe."

Taking charge, Mom and Dad wrangled together some guests to witness the cutting of the cake, which was a small two-tiered one given to Gwen from the people at her old job in the bakery. Then Gwen and The Creep wandered around the twenty guests that were left over and tried to mingle.

I was so exhausted and starving by this time I plopped on an old sofa in the corner and fought back tears.

The soloist, Tom, spotted me on the couch and sat down. He handed me a cloth handkerchief from his pocket.

I blew my nose loudly and sniffed. "Thanks."

"What's the matter?" he asked. "This is supposed to be a happy day."

"I know." I knew he was trying to make me feel better, but at his kind words, I burst into tears and started sobbing. The simple fact was that no one had said more than two words to me the whole day, other than The Creep grabbing my ass and Mom slapping me. And I was tired, hungry, and alone. I wanted to say that I was going to miss Gwen, even if I did hate her. But, I knew I couldn't explain it to Tom without sounding ridiculous. I wanted to say that The Creep was a creep, but knew I wasn't supposed to say anything bad about the family to anyone. And besides, no one would believe me anyway. Instead, I just cried. It didn't matter anyway: I couldn't have told him if I wanted to. I could never talk when I cried. There never seemed enough breath to go around.

Tom stared at me, looking uncomfortable. "Look at it

this way," he said, "you're not losing a sister, you're gaining a brother."

"What?" I shouted, raising my voice. All the left-over guests turned and looked at me. "He's my brother now?" I bawled louder and after handing Tom back his handkerchief, who looked sorry he'd even spoken to me, I ran to the bathroom and hid in a stall, sobbing my eyeballs out.

The full truth of what had just happened smacked me in the face. He was family now. He'd be home for every holiday. He'd be there for special events, or maybe even a family vacation, if we ever took one. He would have free access to comment, ridicule and make fun of me for the rest of my life! He would have a lifetime of opportunities to come after me again, like he had in the kitchen. And all the while, he would make Gwen hate me even more than she already did. For this, I sobbed. I was trapped. I was doomed. There was no escape. I paced the tiny bathroom stall like a caged mountain lion.

I didn't know how long I had been in the bathroom crying. Eventually, my mother came looking for me when it was time to go home. She looked annoyed having found me there, but made no effort to ask me what was wrong. As for me, I was just thankful Mom didn't take the opportunity to yell at me for hiding. I just couldn't have taken it then.

7

PAUL

I shoot hoops at the school until sunset, and then slowly ride my bike home. I figure Mary is home by now, and probably has already gotten her obligatory whipping. I also figure that the rest of the family is sitting around the kitchen table having dinner as if Mary isn't even there, all red-faced and defeated.

I feel sorry for Mary, but every time I think of Gwen the only emotion that rushes to my mind is anger. I'm so pissed at her it hurts. This whole mess is her fault, and she doesn't give a rat's ass whose life she's ruining in the process.

Screw up your own life? Fine!

I stand up on my bike to peddle up the hill from the school and pass Mary's friend's house.

But, it's not just her life Gwen's messing with.

Now, after everything that The Creep and Gwen have done, I'm not Paul Green, the up and coming star on the high school swimming team. I'm the poor freshman with the pregnant, white trash sister. There's not a day that goes by when I'm not teased about it at school. I laugh it off, some of the time, and act like I even agree with what my classmates say; but it cuts. I'm so humiliated. But, most of all, I'm just pissed.

Why doesn't she give the baby up for adoption? I know that the baby will be better off without that moron as his father and a selfish bitch as his mother.

Why did she marry that jerk? Why is she being so stubborn? Why is she giving back a partial scholarship to be a teacher like she's always wanted, in order to be a military wife and a teenage mother? It doesn't make any sense at all! Doesn't she see what it will do to her life? Doesn't she see she'll be working minimum wage jobs forever? Doesn't she realize what it's doing to the rest of the family? Doesn't she get what kind of life the baby is going to have with poor, unskilled parents barely old enough to vote? Does she even understand? Does she care?

And you know what? Even if somebody told her, she wouldn't believe them! She's so friggin' brainwashed she actually thinks she's doing the right thing. Oh my God, Gwen! Wake up!!

Stupid.

I don't figure Gwen cares about anything but herself and what she thinks she wants. I know she's making a royal mess of her life, and it's spilling over, infecting us around her, and it makes me completely ticked off!

Not that I'd say anything about it, though. It won't make any difference anyway.

I peddle up the hill and coast towards the house. I wonder what's for dinner.

After the wedding, Mom, Dad, me, Mary and Rose came home and peeled off our wedding clothes. Mom made a pot of spaghetti for dinner, with bread and butter, and we ate in silence; all except Rose who wanted to talk about how beautiful everybody was at the wedding. But nobody joined her in the conversation.

Mary looked like hell, with her eyes all puffed out and her face splotchy, but I figured it was because of the stress of the day. Mary was always crying these days. Honestly, I didn't know how she kept hydrated.

After dinner, Mom and Dad turned on the TV and we sat down in the family room to watch. It was quiet. Hardly anyone spoke. Mary sat in front of the TV to turn channels. The remote batteries were dead again, but it was determined that there was nothing on worth watching, so Dad popped a movie into the old VCR (since the DVD had been broken for months), and Mom made some popcorn. We passed around small bowls and drank ice cold milk.

At the end of the evening, when the movie was over and Mom and Dad announced it was time for bed, no one objected. No one fought or negotiated for more time. No one yelled or screamed that it was too early. We stood, said good night, brushed our teeth without being told, put on our pajamas or night gowns and went to bed.

I lay for a while in bed, staring at the ceiling. I couldn't figure out why the evening had been so different. We always sat and watched movies together. We always made popcorn and passed around small bowls. Yet, the experience had been so strange, almost like it had not happened at all. It had been so . . . so . . . so . . . what?

I rolled over onto my side and pulled the covers over my shoulders. Was not having Gwen there really that much of a difference? Or was it because everybody was tired after the wedding? If only I could find the right word for what is was. It was . . . it was . . . but before the word came, sleep arrived, and no further thoughts passed through my mind until the next morning.

After a breakfast of Dad's famous French toast, I joined Mary on the side of the house to skateboard. It had been a long time since we'd done that, and I'd forgotten how good she actually was.

She knew the Ollie, and kickturns, and fifty-fifty grinds off those brick walls like it was second nature. I was a bit taken aback.

After lunch Mary went upstairs and played with Rose, so I hooked up the old Sega and had a Sonic tournament with Mom. Dad went about the house and fixed a few things, like the broken light switch in the family room and the timer on the back yard sprinklers.

During that week, it was the first time in a long while that I thought Mary wasn't as annoying. She hadn't cried in a few days, or whined about everything that happened or went wrong. But on the last day, I noticed her slipping back into old habits. She'd gotten up early to skateboard, and whined when it was time to come into breakfast. At lunch, she did the same. She didn't want to come inside, she didn't want to talk, she just wanted to skateboard back and forth in front of the house to the corner of the block, and why did she have to take the trash out now?

Since it was winter, there wasn't much to do at the Recreation Center other than play foosball and shoot some pool, or play tennis. So, I decided to skateboard, too.

By the afternoon, I got the sense Mary wasn't in a talking mood. She wasn't performing any tricks on the side yard, but just rode, back and forth, back and forth in front of the house, and was always ahead of me, not letting me pass.

Finally, near dinner time, I caught up to her. She was

standing on the corner of the block, holding her skateboard in one arm. She was talking to a kid her own age, a boy.

Curious, I rode down to meet them but was not prepared for what came next.

"Are you hungry, Ugly Mary? Want a cookie?" Some prick from Mary's class was grinning like he'd just found the secret to ultimate power. Then he cackled which caused Mary's face to turn bright pink and her eyes to fill with tears.

I felt my blood boil. "What are you laughing at, twerp?"

Mary answered. "He and some boys gave me a cookie with spit all over it."

The kid sneered. "And she ate it, too!" He laughed some more.

But that didn't last long.

In a flash I was off my skateboard, my fist colliding with that prick's nose with a splat. He hit the pavement hard, erupting into an immediate wail.

"Whoa!" Mary gasped, gaping at the blood dripping down the kid's face.

He got up and scrambled back onto his bike. "I'm gonna' tell my dad!" he sobbed. Then he peddled away, wobbling back and forth enough to make Mary laugh.

I looked at Mary, and even though she smiled at me, I couldn't bring myself to smile back. I got back on my skateboard and rode to the house, a sense of dread building in me.

I'd get into trouble now, for sure. Here I was always telling Mary to shut up and I fly off the handle and punch some twelve-year-old. What the hell's the matter with me?

As I suspected, there was a price to pay for losing my temper with that little prick. His name was Jefferson Randall, and the bad news for me was that little Jefferson's father was a lawyer. He called Mom and Dad within minutes of Jeffy's return home, demanding that they pay for his trip to the emergency room, and threatening to call the principals of both my school and Mary's school so that a full-scale investigation could be done when school started again the next day.

I found out later, sure enough, back at school, Mary had been called from class to speak to the principal and had spilled everything. I wasn't surprised Mary had told on me, or to hear Mom start in on Mary for opening her big mouth again. Just a little disappointed.

"Ever hear of something called family loyalty, Mary?" Mom yelled.

"Yes?" Mary half-whispered.

"Then why did you tell Mr. Bozner that Paul punched Jefferson?"

"Because he did? I told the truth, Mom. Was I supposed to lie to the principal?" Mary was visibly shaken and took a step away from Mom.

"You were supposed to be loyal to Paul!"

"So, I should have lied?"

Mom didn't answer that. "You don't get it, Mary."

Mary burst into tears. I stood across the room. To Mary, I knew a comment like that was the greatest insult. "But I told the truth!" she bawled.

"Go to your room and think about it, Mary . . . !" Mom said. In an instant Mary was running past her and half way up the stairs, "Think about family loyalty, and what that means to you, and . . ."

Mary's door slammed.

"Don't slam the door," Mom whispered.

I plopped on the couch. If I'd known punching Jefferson Randall was going to get them both into trouble, I would have broken the kid's bike too. At least then, the punishment would have fit the crime.

The second day after school had started again, Gwen came home from the honeymoon. The instant her feet hit the shag carpet the whirlwind began again.

The first bit of drama occurred over where Gwen was going to live. Before the wedding, The Creep had requested base housing in South Carolina, where he was to be stationed, but they had not heard yet. After the honeymoon, word came that there was no base housing available, and Gwen's hopes of moving out of the house were dashed, just like that. She expressed her displeasure at this every time she opened her mouth.

So, when it came time for The Creep to go back, Gwen stayed because they couldn't afford an off-base apartment. And if I had thought she was unhappy before the wedding, having to stay at home after the wedding made her even worse.

"What is that crap you're listening to, Paul? It's awful!"

"Zepplin." I looked up from the homework spread out in front of me on my desk. Gwen stood in the doorway to my room.

"It's horrid! You must be tone deaf!"

I went back to my homework and said, "That's possible."

"Even Mary plays the violin! You? You're an untalented dork! I don't know how you're a member of the same gene pool!"

This caught my attention. "I've often wondered the same thing." I grasped the remote to the stereo without looking away from her hot eyes and turned up the volume so high the window vibrated.

Gwen cursed at me, but the music was so loud I couldn't hear her, though by the way her lips moved I knew what she had said. "What?" I bellowed, sarcastically cupping my palm to my ear. "I can't hear you!"

Gwen flipped me the bird and stomped away, no doubt to

complain to Mom about my loud music. I turned the music back down to a tolerable decibel and went back to my homework. I could hear Gwen screeching downstairs something about how my music was upsetting her.

Good.

Now that Gwen was home fulltime I could tell Mom and Dad were trying to make the best of it, though they were failing miserably. They encouraged her to study for her G.E.D. so she could get a job as a high school graduate. She was showing a swollen belly, but would be able to work for a few months, at least, in order to save up some money before the baby came. But, whatever Mom and Dad suggested was usually the exact opposite of what Gwen and The Creep chose to do. So, against Mom and Dad's advice, Gwen went back into high school with the intention of graduating with her classmates. This meant that I was attending school with Gwen every day. I sincerely didn't get why she wanted to waddle through those halls, given what everybody was saying about her. But, I can only guess it was to show them she didn't care what they thought.

I knew otherwise.

Plus, now, instead of me being made fun of for having a pregnant teenage sister, I was now getting openly mocked for having a pregnant, teenage and *married* sister.

"Where do you think we are, Green?" a group of seniors

taunted me at swimming practice. "In the back woods of Alabama?"

"We got ourselves a real-life hillbilly!"

"Yee-haw! Let's go huntin' fer some rabbits so's we can eat some supper, Pa!"

"Hold on there, lemme whittle this here spear so's I can pick my only tooth."

More often than not, Coach would shush the crowd and put the seniors to work doing push-ups for being such dolts, but it never stopped them for long. They were at it again the following day, laughing all the way through their push-ups and squealing like they were calling pigs on a farm.

This only added to my fury. To cool off, I disappeared from the house the moment I was no longer grounded. Mom and Dad, who seemed too focused on punishing Mary for blinking, and too preoccupied yelling at Gwen, never seemed to notice I was gone every day after school, and only arrived home for meals, to disappear right afterwards.

I knew I was luckier than Mary, who was trapped at the house. That poor girl couldn't fart without getting into trouble. It seemed to me Mom and Dad were over punishing Mary in order to squelch any rebellious thoughts before they entered her mind, so as not to create another Gwen. But even I could tell they were going about it the wrong way.

Meanwhile, when Mary wasn't crying over some unfair punishment from Mom and Dad, she was getting it from Gwen, who was on a special mission to make her cry at least once a day. The worse Mary felt, the worse she behaved, and the more she got into trouble. Which sucked for her.

Gwen told Mary she was useless and would never amount to anything, over and over. When it got really bad, and even I couldn't listen to it anymore, I'd leave again. There was no point in telling Gwen to stop. She would only turn her venom on me, and I wanted to pummel that whacked-out bitch, so it was best if I just left without a word.

I knew Mary was stuck, having had her bike and skateboard taken away for being mean to Rose, or lying about some such stupid thing, like if she'd eaten the last of the chips and put the empty bag back in the pantry. But I couldn't worry about her. I had to get out of there before I did something to Gwen. I was *that* angry.

Some days I'd leave with Gwen screaming at Mary, only to return to dinner and hear the same thing.

"Stop slouching and sit up straight!"

"Your hair's a mess! Did you even brush it today?"

"Your breath smells like there's a dead dog in your mouth! Go brush your teeth!"

"What are you wearing? You look like a cow! I can't believe you'd go out in public like that!"

"When you squat like that I can see the rolls of fat on your stomach!"

"You're eating again? Oink, oink!"

"Quit squirming; can't you sit still?"

"Stop humming; you sound like a sick moose!"

"You forgot to close the shower curtain again! Can't you do anything right?"

"Your shoelace is untied! Honestly, Mary, you're such a disaster!"

Day after day. Hour after hour.

Minute upon minute.

Finally, one day, Mary disappeared for a few hours, and by accident I walked in on her hiding in the bathtub, the shower curtain closed. I found her because I heard her crying.

When I pulled back the curtain she hardly even looked up at me. She had her knees pressed tightly against her chest and was rocking back and forth like a lunatic. She was staring at something in front of her, tears crusted down her cheeks. When I reached down and snatched what she was so focused on, she seemed to snap out of it.

"Gimme that!" she squealed, swiping her hands in the air, trying to get it back.

It was a bottle of aspirin.

I put the aspirin back into the medicine cabinet. "You'd

better clean out the tub when you get out of there. If Mom sees those dirty sneaker marks, she'll freak."

I left with Mary still in the tub. I heard the shower curtain close again as I rounded the corner.

She must have a whopper headache from all the crying. Poor kid's losing it.

The moment I enter the front door I can tell Mary isn't back yet. Dad's home, for one, and Mom has Rose wearing a jacket and holding a flashlight. When Mom sees me she looks hopeful.

I shake my head, and the deep frown returns to Mom's face. "Did you see Mary, Paulie?" *Rose asks.*

"No."

"Mom says she's going to get the whipping of a lifetime when she finds her!" Rose says. She grins. She's missing her two front teeth and a few on the bottom. She looks like a pink jack-o-lantern. Having received so few whippings herself, Rose obviously doesn't have any idea how bad it is. I hope she never does.

"If we find her," I mumble, passing them into the family room.

"What?" Rose looks horror struck. "What does he mean, Mommy? We are *going to find her, aren't we? Aren't we?"*

"Shush for a minute," Mom says.

Dad arrives from the garage and hands her another flash-

light, which Mom turns on and off to test. "Paul, did you check the Recreation Center while you were out?"

"No." I plop down on the couch.

"Aren't we?" Rose whines.

"I called Tammy's." Mom zips her jacket. "Miriam will call if she shows up."

"All right," Dad says, "Paul and I got the Rec Center, and around the neighborhood. You take the school, the park and Tammy's. Maybe she's hiding in a bush someplace."

"Aren't we?" Rose interjects.

"Yes, yes," Mom says, rolling her eyes,

Gwen arrives during this. "Look, I don't know why you're making such a big deal of this. When she gets hungry, she'll come home. She couldn't have gotten far. And it's not like she's smart enough to have taken any money with her for bus fare. I say let's go to dinner. How much you want to bet by the time we get home, she'll be on the front porch begging to be let in?"

Nobody responds to Gwen. I'm beginning to notice a new pattern of communication amongst the family. If they don't agree with you, they simply say nothing. Out-right telling Gwen they don't agree would cause a roar of shouting and crying from the new mother, and Mom and Dad are done with that. So, they say nothing, as if they haven't heard Gwen at all. And Gwen, who is too self-involved to really care about *anything else, figures they agree with her, and turns to sit on the couch.*

"I'm in the mood for Chinese," she says.

Mom opens her mouth to speak, and closes it again. I know why. It's too much effort to speak to Gwen.

Anything spoken she takes out of context, dissects to mean something entirely different than what is meant, twists it, harps upon it and shouts about it. A person has to think long and hard about what he or she says to Gwen, and at this time, with Mary missing, Mom opts wisely to say nothing more to her eldest daughter. After all, she's spent the last year talking until she's blue in the face, and look where that's gotten us.

8

MARY

I have a plan. In my mind, there is no other option. This has to work. Despite what the entire world thinks of me, I know I can work hard. I'm not lazy. I know I'm not especially smart, but I can do a hard day's work.

So, when I enter the mall from the front glass doors, and the smell of floor wax, window cleaner and plastic greet me, I know that someplace in this mall is the solution to my problem.

I will get a job. I'll earn my own money and rent a room from one of my co-workers. I know this is far-fetched, but I will convince them to make an exception.

I have to do this before dark because I'm not sure where I'm going to stay the night. I'm not going home, and it's already dark outside. If push comes to shove, I'll hide in one of the bathrooms when the mall closes and sleep on one of the mattresses in Macy's.

I pass the movie theater and decide I can't work there; my family might go to the movies, and I don't ever want to see them again. I don't want the yogurt shop either – it's right next to the movie theater and too risky. The Gap is next to the yogurt shop, but Mom bought me a shirt there once, so that's out as well.

I'm a little concerned that this is going to be a more difficult task than I originally thought. I smooth out my tee shirt, put on my sweatshirt and zip it, and run my fingers through my hair. I have to look presentable. This is my only chance and I don't want to blow it like I do everything else. It's this, or the aspirin bottle.

A few months after the wedding, I heard that The Creep got transferred to a base in Tennessee where he was going to fix car air conditioners. At first, Gwen had proudly announced to the family that The Creep was going through special training to be a guard at the White House, and that they'd be moving to Washington D.C., but a few weeks later he was sent back to fixing air conditioners without any further explanation from Gwen. I heard Mom and Dad talking in private about what they thought happened – that the "punk had failed the 'psych' test, or got kicked out for his bad attitude, or maybe the whole thing was a lie" – but they didn't bother to ask Gwen. Mom and Dad had given up trying to get the truth from her. The good news in all that, Gwen informed the family, was that in Tennessee there was plenty of base housing so, for the first time, Gwen got to live with her husband.

I noticed immediately the change in Gwen. Gwen was so happy, her entire personality changed. Suddenly, she wasn't the miserable, whining, cranky and moody wench, but calm, excited and full of joy.

I guess it was because Gwen was finally getting what she wanted. What a brat.

Because of this new sense of happiness, I think picking on her worthless little sister became a low priority in Gwen's life. I wasn't sure I could trust the new-found quiet, but enjoyed having a teeny bit of leeway. Gwen went about packing all her things, took and passed the G.E.D., dropped out of high school for the last time, said good bye to what few friends she had left, and Mom and Dad somehow got the money to pay for Gwen's one-way plane ticket to Tennessee.

Within days of The Creep's transfer it was time for Gwen to join him. On the morning of her departure, Gwen stopped me on my way out the door to school and handed me a pair of turquoise and silver unicorn earrings.

I stared at the earrings in my palm, and then at my sister. I couldn't believe someone who obviously hated me so much was being that nice. Something had to be wrong.

"Really? I get to keep them?" I asked.

"Yes, silly! I know you like horses so I figured . . . there you go! Here, let me help you put them in." Gwen reached for me. I flinched.

"Hold still," Gwen said patiently. I couldn't believe my ears.

Who was this person, and what had she done with my sister?

When Gwen was done putting the earrings in, she smoothed my lumpy hair over my ears and gave me a quick hug.

"Take care of Rosie, okay?" Gwen's voiced cracked, and to my complete shock, tears were in Gwen's eyes; and for once, they weren't tears of rage.

"Um, okay," I said.

"Alright. Bye!" Gwen turned and walked briskly away, towards her room, leaving me in the foyer, thunderstruck. Eventually, Rose came into the foyer and I came to my senses. Together, we began the walk to school.

On the way, I silently replayed the scene with Gwen over and over, trying to figure out why Gwen had behaved so strangely. Suddenly, a thought hit me. Had Gwen been trying to be nice? But, why would she do that? What did Gwen have to gain by being nice to me now? What was her angle?

The more my thoughts swam, the more confused I got. The one thing I kept coming back to was that Gwen had been nice, and now she was moving away. Just when she got to be nice, she leaves? The utter unfairness slapped me in the face.

Emotions rushed at me, blurring my vision and burning my eyes. She was nice, and she's leaving!

"Mary, what's wrong?" Rose asked, watching me. "Forget it, Rose."

Rose moved a little closer and pointed at my wet face. "You're crying!"

"I am not. Just be quiet!" I walked ahead, wiping my eyes on the sleeve of my sweatshirt tied around my waist.

"Why are you crying, Mary?" Rose persisted.

"Will you leave me alone?"

"Not until you tell me why you're crying!" Rose crossed her arms across her chest.

I saw Rose's posture and had a cruel idea. My tears instantly dried. "Gwen is moving away today."

"What?" Rose stopped in her tracks.

"Gwen's moving out forever," I snarled, hardly slowing down.

Rose's face fell. "That's not true! Mom said it was just for a little while!"

"She lied," I spat the words like venom, "to make you feel better."

"But, where is she going?" Rose asked, her voice sounding small and defeated.

"Tennessee."

"Forever?" Rose's eyes were teeming with tears.

I refused to notice. I was at least a yard ahead. I could hear the tears in Rose's voice, but couldn't stop myself from pouring salt on the wound. For once, I was not the one being made to feel miserable.

So there!

It felt marvelous. "Yep," I said, "forever."

"But, but . . . maybe it's just for a little while?" Rose had sprinted ahead and was now just behind me.

"Nope, it's forever."

"Oh no!" Rose's sobs grew louder. "Really?"

"Yep!"

Rose cried all the way to school, and for a moment, I forgot my own feelings. It didn't last long.

To enter the school you had to walk through the lower grade playground first. When we arrived onto the school yard, Rose was immediately surrounded by a group of concerned friends, who comforted her and walked her over to one of the school yard teachers. I stood and watched them rub her back, give her hugs and offer her the napkins from their lunch boxes to blow her nose and felt sick with envy and shame.

I spent the remaining minutes before class in the upper grade bathroom, sniffling and blowing my nose on the hard brown sheets of paper towel, then biting my lower lip as I sat down at my desk after the bell rang.

"Hey, Mary, why are you crying?" This time it was Tammy asking, more curious than concerned, and I didn't mind. I was hoping for a little of the treatment Rose had gotten from her friends. Tammy's desk was one row in front of mine, and Tammy had turned all the way around for our morning greeting to see me looking like a red swollen mess.

"Gwen is moving away today."

"Oh," Tammy said, pursing her lips in confusion then turning back around in her seat to face the blackboard.

I sighed and felt sick to my stomach. There was no hug, no tissues, no nothing. I knew why, though. I couldn't blame Tammy for not understanding how I felt. Tammy probably couldn't figure out why I was sad when all I ever did was complain about Gwen.

"Does this mean you get her room?" Tammy asked, turning around with an excited expression.

Much to my horror, I was unable to contain the tears, and burst into a loud sob.

Gwen had been nice to me!

I wanted Gwen to stay if she wasn't going to make me feel badly all the time about everything!

Overcome, I ran outside the classroom and closed the door, hiding behind a wall just outside. I thought of all the sisterly things Gwen and I could have done, or could do someday, like go shopping, or to the pool, or the Recreation Center to play foosball. Maybe Gwen could do my hair like she did for Rose.

Rose. My stomach churned with sourness. I had treated Rose just like Gwen had always treated me. And I'd liked it! I was a terrible, awful sister, just like Gwen used to be.

But, Gwen was nice now! And it was too late to do anything about it, because now, Gwen was in Tennessee, and it was too late for me to have the older sister I'd always wanted.

I didn't know how long I'd stayed outside crying. Eventually, when I went back inside, the teacher, Mrs. Chastain, didn't ask where I had been. I figured I was so unimportant the teacher hadn't noticed I was gone.

This was no surprise.

That afternoon after school, I came home to a silent house. No one said much during dinner, and hardly anyone spoke that night in front of the TV. After a few days like that, however, the quiet grew to be normal, and not as loud. If that makes any sense.

Without Gwen there to constantly nag at me, I got to thinking about other things, and not so much about how horrible I was.

In fact, I wondered why I hadn't written any stories for a long time, and sat down to write one. In an hour, I'd written three. I was so happy about this, I took out my homework, and did that, too. Doing homework was a lot easier than I remembered.

A week after that, Tammy and I did a report on eclipses (which I admit, Tammy did most of the work on), but we got a good grade and I liked the way that felt. I decided I wanted to get more good grades.

It turned out a surprise to me, but if I listened to Mrs. Chastain, and did the work she sent home, I knew the test answers. I felt like I'd figured out some sort of secret formula to success, and that I was somehow cheating. Why hadn't anyone told me this before?

After a week or two of this, I was doing so well in school that Mrs. Chastain asked me to join the Academic Pentathlon team. The Pentathlon team got to go to another school and take tests with other kids in the district. Whoever did the best on the tests got a trophy. The tests were going to be about outer space, and Mrs. Chastain said since Tammy's and my report was on eclipses, she thought I'd like to be on the team.

I was so excited, I told Mrs. Chastain that I wanted to join, even if it meant extra homework. A newspaper reporter took the team's picture. Mom was so proud she cut out the article with my picture and put it on the refrigerator.

The other thing I didn't mind so much anymore was practicing my violin. Mom's yelling from the bottom of the stairs didn't bother me; and besides, Mom wasn't yelling as much on the whole.

"I heard from the music teacher at your school that the Honor Orchestra is having auditions soon," Mom said to me one day as we were standing together holding our violins, having just played the "Upside Down" duet by Mozart, as I called it. "I think if you play the Mlynarski Mazurka you would do really well. What do you think?"

I looked at Mom's hopeful face and felt an overwhelming urge to please her. "Sure. Okay."

"Great!" Mom said, turning to her file cabinet and pulling out three pages of music. "We should get started then."

For months, Mom and I practiced together. For me, it was a chance to hang out with Mom, who didn't seem to hate me as much as she used to. It felt nice that something I did was able to please her. It had been a long time since I'd felt like that.

When the audition day arrived, Mom drove me to the

junior high campus, and every violin player from all the schools in the entire district were there. When it was my turn, I was so nervous my hands went clammy. I played the Mazurka for the four judges, and they gave me a piece of music to sight read. The song they picked was easy, and one I'd played before.

After the audition, Mom took me to Baskin Robbins, and I got to have a double scoop on a sugar cone.

I waited a few days and then a letter came in the mail. It was addressed to "The Parents of Mary Green," from The District Honor Orchestra, so I immediately took the letter to Mom, who was hunched over the sewing machine in the garage, under an old desk lamp Dad had screwed into the wall, hemming an old dress of mine for Rose.

"Mom?"

She didn't look up from the machine, and her foot didn't ease up on the pedal. "Yes."

"I got the letter." For some reason, I got extremely nervous all of the sudden. I knew I'd done well at the audition. I even knew that the Mazurka was a hard piece to play, and that I'd played it the best I could. However, it occurred to me just then that perhaps I hadn't gotten into the orchestra at all, and how Mom's face would look when I read the letter giving the bad news. I imagined how Mom would sigh that disappointed sigh she always gave me, and then turn back to the sewing without saying a word. At least, that's how I saw it happening. Now, I wished I'd opened it up and checked first.

"The letter?" The sewing machine strained over the hem and hummed for a moment.

"From the Orchestra," I said.

The sewing machine stopped and Mom's eyes turned from behind her glasses, peering at me with a squint. "Did you open it?"

"It says, 'To the parents of Mary Green,' so no."

Mom sat up in her chair and contemplated for a moment. "Go ahead."

With trembling fingers I opened the letter and cleared my throat to read it aloud. "Congratulations, your child has been accepted into the Capistrano Valley Elementary School District Honor Orchestra. . . ."

In a rush, Mom pushed back the metal folding chair with a loud scraping noise and I lowered the letter and jumped back. Before I could even see the expression on Mom's face, I was in her arms, smothered between Mom's belly and breasts.

"Well done, Mary," Mom said. "I'm so proud of you." And just like that Mom let me go, and left the garage.

I needed to sit down. I stumbled to the folding chair and

collapsed, still holding the letter in my hands. Mom's words echoed in my head repeatedly. I could hear my heart beating in my ears.

I'm so proud of you.

The letter went on the refrigerator next to the newspaper article. When the day came for rehearsals to start, I got out of school early and took the bus to the junior high. I walked into the concert hall to find the chair with my name on it. I went through the second violin section, where all the mediocre players sat, but couldn't find my name. So, I went to the back of the first violin section where the better players sat, and couldn't find it there either. Right about the time I got worried they had sent me the wrong letter, I went to the first chair position, which is usually reserved for the very best player in the entire orchestra, and stood there shocked as I read my name.

First chair! First chair!!

That meant I was the best out of the whole group. I was the number one best player out of them all! In the entire district! Resisting the urge to squeal and jump up and down, I sat in my chair, shakily took out my violin, tuned it by ear and rosined my bow.

First chair! First chair!!

Wait 'til Mom hears about this!

After rehearsal, I waited in the front of the school by the

parking lot. When our clunky maroon station wagon pulled up, I had only one thing on my mind. I was barely in the door with it closed behind me before I started shouting.

"First chair, Mom! I'm first chair!"

"Of the first violins?" Mom asked.

"Yes! Can you believe it?"

Rose was in the back seat of the car; she leaned forward. "What's first chair?"

"Wow, Mary! Well done!" Mom said, pulling the car forward so the other cars behind her could get to the curb.

"What's first chair?" Rose asked again.

"I think this deserves a celebration," Mom said, pulling out of the parking lot.

"Pizza! Pizza!" Rose was so excited, she was bobbing up and down.

"Pizza or ice cream, Mary?" Mom asked.

"Ice cream!"

"That's what I thought." She turned the car and headed straight to Baskin Robbins, even though it was dinner time, and I wondered who in their right mind would ever turn down ice cream for dinner?

My lucky streak didn't end there. In addition to the Pentathlon Team and the Honor Orchestra, I tried out for the school softball team and got on the team! I was at second base, and to my surprise, despite never having a batting lesson in my life, was a good hitter. We practiced during recess every Friday and got to play the teachers in a game at the end of the year. Not everybody in the sixth grade got to be on the team, so it was a big deal. Mrs. Mayes from the sixth grade class next door was my coach. She was always very nice to me. When I told Dad I got on the team he said he would take off work so he could come see the game when it was time. That made my day. Dad never took off from work for anything.

Feeling particularly brave one day after school, I snuck into Gwen's old room and collected a bunch of books and took them to my room. After browsing a few of the titles, I settled on an old Nancy Drew mystery that had been Mom's and ended up reading until dark. I loved it. My parents had to threaten me to get me to come to dinner.

"What have you been doing up there, Mary?"

"Reading."

For some odd reason, I didn't get yelled at for being late.

Later, at school, I convinced the old members of The Pretend Club to rejoin and scripted fantastical stories for them to act out based on the books I had read.

Life was good. For the first time in a while, I felt happy and did not consider for one second why. I just enjoyed it.

After a few more weeks of this normal life, my dark cloud

evaporated. I didn't feel so gloomy all the time. I was on top of the world. If I'd taken the time to notice then, I may have seen that the entire family was caught under the same spell.

Dinner was fun now. We joked and laughed, had burping contests, and told funny stories about how our days went. I started watching this spy show on TV and became obsessed with it, reading all about the episodes in magazines and pinning pictures of the lead actor on the wall by my bed. And I guess because it made me so happy, my family didn't mind watching the show with me when it was on.

Things changed for Paul, too. He was asked to try out for the water polo team in the Spring. Coach Sands thought Paul showed real promise, even as a freshman, so he asked Paul to try out. The whole family went together to the Recreation Center where Paul swam laps and treaded water holding a milk jug full of water over his head. A few days later he got a letter saying he got on the team and his practices were to start the next Monday before school. That meant Paul couldn't take the bus to school anymore because he had to go to the Recreation Center first, but Mom said she didn't mind the extra drive. Dad was so proud, he saved up some money so Paul could buy himself a letterman's jacket. Paul was only on the Junior Varsity team as an alternate, but Dad bought him the jacket anyway and Mom stitched on the giant 'JV' by hand.

Things looked to be going pretty well when we got a phone call from Gwen. We hadn't heard from her at all after she had gone, and despite the fact that Mom and Dad jumped and ran to the phone every time it rang, they seemed surprised when she actually called. The Creep was being sent to South Carolina to repeat training, Gwen said, and there still wasn't any base housing available there which meant Gwen needed to move back home. Mom and Dad thought this was probably for the best since Gwen was far along into the pregnancy.

At first, I was excited about Gwen coming home. I mean, after all, she was nice now!

Mom and Dad helped me clean up Gwen's room and we went to the consignment store and got a used bassinette for when the baby was born.

We all went together to pick up Gwen from the airport. To our surprise, Gwen looked neither happy to see us, nor anything like her old self. She was almost unrecognizable. Now eight months along in her pregnancy, Gwen's legs were round and thick like tree trunks, her ankles were swollen and spotted like giant polish sausages, and none of her shoes fit anymore. She waddled and slapped around the airport wearing The Creep's old flip flops. The little round belly she had when she left now looked like she had an overblown basketball stuffed under her shirt. Her shirt was too small, so her belly hung out of the bottom, and her pants were so tight, the seams stretched almost to the point of bursting. Her face was oily and covered in pimples, and her hair was stuck to her scalp, like it hadn't been washed in weeks.

When Gwen arrived at the house she took a long, hot shower and propped her feet up on the coffee table in the family room, wrapped in Dad's gigantic bathrobe.

I popped in a taped episode of my favorite spy show for Gwen, who apparently did not have a TV in Tennessee, and was hoping to convert another family member in my quest to never miss an episode when Mom arrived, having just gotten off the phone with Gwen's doctor.

"Gwen, Dr. Murdoch has an opening in a half hour, so get dressed and I'll take you."

"Forget it! I just got off an airplane and you expect me to run across town now?"

There was a moment of stunned silence from both Mom and me. It had been so long since we'd heard screaming like that, that it seemed out of place. It was like Gwen had spoken a different language and we sat with our heads turned to one side trying to understand what she had said.

"Why are you screaming?" Mom asked.

"I'm not screaming! I'm exhausted, and I'm not going to get poked and prodded by that old geezer if I don't need to! Besides, I just sat down!"

"Actually, you've been sitting there for a whole hour," I said, pointing to the TV.

"Oh, shut up, stupid. Who asked you?"

I felt like I'd been slapped. Any illusions I'd had about my sisterly relationship with Gwen were gone at that very moment. I looked at Mom and saw red splotches spread across her chest and her face go white. I knew Mom had just remembered, too. I didn't say anything else, and went to my room like I used to do when Gwen was mean to me. Only this time, I didn't feel sad or hurt by her mean words. This time, I was mad!

How dare she!

I punched my pillow a few times, and when that didn't make me feel any better, I smacked around a few stuffed animals.

How dare she!

"Mary, what are you doing?" Rose was watching me.

"Mind your own beeswax!" I snarled, and I did it so meanly that Rose ran out of the room.

Who does Gwen think she is?

Rose was probably on her way to tattle to Mom, but I didn't care.

Let Mom slap me for being mean to Rose! Let her whip me! At least those bruises faded.

I hate Gwen! I hate her!

I stomped across my bedroom and turned up some music

as loudly as I could, burying my face in my pillow so I could scream as I lay on my bed. When I finished that, I pulled out my diary from under my bed and wrote how much I hated Gwen. I used every curse word I knew. I didn't think Gwen was nice anymore. I knew better. In fact, I thought Gwen was the worst person I'd ever met in my whole life, and I didn't care who knew it.

Hours later, after I'd cooled off, I came back downstairs and heard that Mom had gotten Gwen to go to the doctor, and that it was a good thing she had. Apparently, Gwen's blood pressure was too high and they were concerned about her and the baby. She had gained too much weight while she was gone and they tested her for gestational diabetes, which is the kind you can only get when you are pregnant. Since Grandma Maggie and Grandpa Henry both were diabetics, there was reason to worry. Gwen was told to stay in bed, which instantly made Mom into Gwen's slave.

Gwen had only a few weeks left before the baby was due, but the idea of being stuck on the couch twenty-four/seven returned Gwen to her regular state of bitchiness. Every word from Gwen's mouth was a complaint, a whine, a yell or an insult. She went back to screaming at everybody for everything, and that included making fun of me.

"Move your fat head. You're always in the way!" Gwen screamed at me as she sat in front of the TV.

"You move!" I spat back, feeling a brief rush.

"Shut up, you stupid oaf! How insensitive can you be? Here I am, bedridden, and you're making fun of me because I can't move? What's the matter with you?"

I felt the rush disappear. I didn't want to take Gwen's mouth without fighting back, but all it seemed to do was make it last longer.

The more I fought, the worse Gwen gave it back. Gwen had years of yelling practice over me, and was far better at it, and though I felt an instant happiness in telling Gwen to 'stuff it,' Gwen merely upped her game, tearing me to shreds with her words, causing my anger to boil over.

"Get out of the bathroom, you hog!" Gwen bellowed, pounding on the door.

"There are other people in this house who need to pee!" I shouted back.

"Yes, but you don't have a twenty pound baby sitting on your bladder, so move your lazy ass and get out of the friggin' bathroom!" Gwen yelled back.

Having no argument to this, I quickly pulled up my pants and left the bathroom.

"Didn't you wash your hands? Ew. Oh my God, Mary, you're so disgusting!"

There was no winning. No matter how I looked at it. And when I realized it each time, I'd get pissed off and start crying again. The lump in my throat would suck up all the air in the room, and that stopped me from saying another word. It felt worse than if I'd just taken the abuse from Gwen and shut up.

It happened again and again, and each time my family would watch my defeat and do nothing about it, which made me feel worse yet.

Dad grew so sick and tired of the screaming; I would watch as he got up in the middle of a conversation and traipse out the front door. He'd disappear for a long time, hours even. And when asked by Mom about where he'd gone, he'd say he'd gone for a walk.

He'd landed a new full-time job, finally, so money wasn't as tight as before, but he had taken a heavy pay cut and wasn't happy about it. It didn't help that home was a war zone, either. When he wasn't working, he'd try to keep busy doing little things to fix up the rental house, but Mom insisted it was pointless because the landlady was so mean, she would never give us credit for the improvements and would never pay us back for the supplies. And even though he was doing something, he couldn't shut off his ears and would still hear the screaming. So, he went on more walks, hiding from everything. I wished he'd asked me to go with him.

This left Mom alone with screaming Gwen, and Mom was a mess. Her already short fuse became invisible. Though

I tried to avoid talking to Mom as much as possible, there were times it couldn't be avoided. She was a volcano, waiting to erupt at the slightest thing, and often did.

One night, Mom got so pissed at me for not going to sleep and for talking to Rose, she stormed into our bedroom holding a wire fly swatter in one hand. She slapped the light on.

"All I ask of you is one thing!" Mom had a wild flare in her eyes, and with dark bags under them. She looked like a crazy Muppet. She waved the fly swatter around like it was a part of her arm. "One thing! How hard is it to just listen to me?"

She stomped to the lower bunk and ripped back my sheets. "Mom! No! I'm sorry! I'm sorry!" I curled into a ball, covering my head.

"Go! . . . to! . . . Sleep!" With each word she slashed me across the back of my legs with the wire fly swatter handle.

I didn't hear a word from Rose, who was in the bunk above.

The back of my legs burned like I'd sat on a barbeque. I heard the light switch slap off and the door slam.

In the dark, I cried. I didn't dare move. When I finally stopped bawling, I heard Rose moving above me.

"Mary?"

"Shut up!" I whispered. The back of my thighs hurt so badly I reached around to touch them. They were warm and wet. I knew I hadn't peed, so I got up and turned on the light. When I swiped my palm across the back of my thighs, they came up red with blood.

Oh my god.

I craned my body, trying to see the back of my thighs. Three large, bloody handle-shaped welts were across them; two on the left, one on the right.

I'd been spanked many times before. One time, Mom had broken a wooden spoon on my butt which had caused a large yellow and purple bruise, but there had never been blood.

I stared at the palm of my hand, frozen. If I crawled back into bed I would get blood on my sheets and would most likely get punished for that. So, I did the only thing I thought I could do. I opened the door, and called for my mother.

"Mom?" It barely came out as a whisper. I cleared my throat a little and tried to sound like I hadn't been crying. "Mom?"

I stood holding my palm in front of me for a few seconds, but I didn't hear any voices from downstairs, though I could hear the TV was on.

"Mom?" I raised my voice just a little. "Mom? I'm bleeding, what should I do?"

Rose shushed me loudly. "Don't call her back!"

"Shhh!" I hissed back at her as I stood and waited for Mom to come upstairs and help me. I waited five seconds.

Nothing.

Five seconds more. Nothing, still.

Too afraid to yell any louder, I tiptoed down the stairs, listening.

I heard harsh whispers from the family room.

"What's the matter with you! A wire fly swatter?" Dad sounded angry, which surprised me. I bet he was getting ready to take another walk.

"It's nine thirty, Dennis. And she has school tomorrow!"

"So, you think beating her will help her calm down and go to sleep? How does that make sense?"

"I don't know what else to do," Mom said, and she sounded really sad.

There was an aggravated sigh from Dad, and a rustling, which sent me back upstairs with a scramble. I tried to see the cuts in the bathroom mirror. But it was too dark, and I didn't want to turn on the light. Instead, I rolled off a chunk of toilet paper. The cuts had already stopped bleeding, though my hand had smeared the blood across my pasty skin in streaks. I wiped my hands off, and patted the back of my thighs, then put the bloody tissues in the toilet. I didn't flush, not wanting to give away that I was out of bed.

When I lay down in bed, I rolled onto my stomach, to avoid touching the sheets with the blood. Rose leaned over from the top bunk.

"Mary?"

I turned my face to the wall and yanked the sheets over my head. "Just shut up, Rose."

I was numb. I didn't know what to think anymore. Despite the burning on the back of my thighs, the rest of me was empty. I felt glad Dad said something, but at the same time, I was so afraid of mom hating me. What if Dad sticking up for me made her hate me more? It was an odd jumble of feelings in my poor, stupid head. I could seriously cause my brain to implode and shut down.

One thing was for sure: if only I'd not been talking in bed, none of this would have happened. What had we even been talking about, anyway? I couldn't remember. Was it so important I had to talk about it at bedtime? I was being punished, again, for opening my big, rotten mouth. If only I could sew that blasted thing shut.

It seemed like the room got darker. I felt worse than ever before, before Gwen had left, even. I wasn't a part of this family. Not really. I was lower than the dog. Nobody really wanted me there. I was useless Mary. Ugly Mary. Stupid Mary. Nobody Mary. Nobody.

What else was new?

9

MARY

After much thinking and a full twenty minutes of mental preparation, I enter a children's clothing store called Children's Place because there is a Cashier Wanted *sign stuck to the front on these gigantic glass walls that allow people to see the whole inside of the store. It's perfect because it's hidden in the back corner of the mall by the Shoe Repair kiosk and the See's Candy Shop that only gets busy on Mother's Day and Christmas.*

I go to the front desk where the cash register sits and ask the cute teenage boy working behind the counter, as dignified as I can, if I can have an application.

After giving me the once over, he brushes his long brown bangs away from his blue eyes and asks, "How old are you?"

For a moment I debate lying. But for some unknown reason, I feel the overwhelming urge to tell somebody the truth. "Twelve," I say. "I turn thirteen in a few weeks." My birthday is actually a few months off. That part I stretch.

The boy smiles and a deep set of grooves appear in his cheeks on either side of his mouth. "I'm really sorry," he says, "but you have to be at least fifteen and get your parents to sign a worker's permit before you can get a job."

"Oh, I know. I have a signed form. I just didn't bring it with me."

This part is a total lie. I know about the work permits, but I also know how to forge mom's signature.

"Even with the signature. You have to prove you're fifteen, with like, a school i.d. or something. Do you have one?"

My plans fall apart. This isn't going well. I debate going to a different store, but the boy reads my mind.

"It's the same in all the stores."

The words land on me hard. So hard, in fact, that the wind is knocked from my lungs. I can't get a job anywhere. I guess I'm sleeping in the Macy's instead. I swallow and whisper, "Thanks."

The boy nods, a little confused by my reaction. He looks so honest in his concern, my mouth opens by itself, and my eyes fill with tears.

Plan B.

By a stroke of really bad luck, the school Jog-a-thon was the day after I'd been whipped with the fly swatter. I wore my pink and purple running shorts because the whole purpose of the Jog-a-thon was to run around the field as many times as you could so people would give the school money. The back of my thighs had scabs from the fly swatter handle on them, but I didn't think about that when I got dressed in the morning.

The first few laps passed with no big deal. With each lap the parent volunteer for my class (it was Tammy' mom, of course), would punch another hole in the paper plate around my neck to record the laps, and I would set off again. There was no hurry, so I jogged along, taking my time.

About half way through the hour, I noticed Mrs. Mayes from the softball team was running behind me.

"What happened to the back of your legs, Mary?" she asked.

I'd forgotten about the welts until then. "Oh," I said, fumbling with what to say, "I don't know."

I knew it was a bad lie the moment it came out. Mrs.

Mayes didn't say anything more, however, so I just kept on running.

I ran a long time, and to my surprise, I ended up winning fourth place. Principal Bozner gave me a little trophy with a golden girl running on the top during a school assembly that afternoon. I took the award and smiled at the crowd of kids as they clapped, but was more concerned that someone would see the back of my legs and laugh.

After school that day Mrs. Chastain asked me to stay.

"Mary," Mrs. Chastain said. "I've realized over the last few weeks you've stopped turning in your homework, your test scores are down, and you aren't turning in your extra work for the Pentathlon Team."

I didn't know what to say to this. It was true. Since Gwen had been home I just didn't feel like it anymore. So, I stood there like a dummy.

Mrs. Chastain stared a long time as if she was waiting for me to say something. Finally, the teacher lowered her face and asked, "Is everything alright at home?"

In an instant, I was crying again. I was so tired of crying all the time! In a rush of happiness, I decided then and there Mrs. Chastain was the greatest teacher in the whole world, because she'd seen I was unhappy. Finally, I could tell the truth! I tried to talk, but was having a hard time catching my breath. All I managed to squeak out was, "I . . . can't . . . do . . . anything . . . right."

There! It was out! I let out the heaviest sigh of relief. It was all going to change now. I could feel it!

The soft expression on Mrs. Chastain's face suddenly changed, and a weird smile crossed her lips. She shook her head.

As Mrs. Chastain struggled for the correct words, I watched her, completely confused. This wasn't the response I'd expected at all. I tried to catch my breath between choked sobs so I could explain what I'd meant, but Mrs. Chastain found her words first.

"Oh," Mrs. Chastain said, "we're in this phase, are we?"

My mouth slammed shut as I thought about what Mrs. Chastain had said. Was she making fun of me? But . . . but . . . she understood, didn't she?

I just told her I couldn't do anything right and she thinks I'm joking?

The tears instantly dried from my eyes as I ate my humiliation whole.

I'm not joking!

My heart thumped against my chest and I had a sudden urge to throw up.

Oh my god, I can't even tell my teacher right!

I hadn't a clue what to say to Mrs. Chastain to explain to her. The teacher looking at me just like Gwen did, whenever I came in a room, like she was sorry for me, like she was looking at a stupid, ugly dog begging for a bone. Like, "Get away, you mangy mutt!"

I just stood there, shaking, so full of emotion I got lost in them. Mrs. Chastain sighed and moved some papers around on her desk. "I gave you a spot on the Pentathlon team thinking it would spark more effort out of you, but it hasn't. If you don't get it together, Mary, you'll be removed from the team. I have many other kids who would love this opportunity. Understood?"

I shook my head 'no' but Mrs. Chastain's eyes were back to the papers on her desk.

"You can go," Mrs. Chastain said.

For a moment, I thought I'd try and explain again. I hesitated in front of the teacher's desk, on the cusp of spilling my guts. But, Mrs. Chastain's head was down, her expression was hard, and I knew I'd blown it.

As always.

I snatched my backpack from under my desk and when I got outside, Tammy was waiting for me.

"What happened?" she asked.

I was so upset I couldn't form two words. "Nothing."

I walked off in the opposite direction. I was crying so

hard, I forgot to pull the tabs on my backpack straps loose so that it hung down past my bottom, to hide the cuts on the back of my thighs as I walked away.

I gape at the boy in Children's Place and barely blinking, mutter a weak, "Okay."

I have no choice now. No job. Sleep in Macy's.

Past the See's Candy Shop and the shoe repair kiosk, there's the Macy's. I go inside and walk around the mattresses for a while before I realize I'm an idiot. Everything Gwen ever said about me is right. There aren't any bathrooms by the mattresses and the sales people in the mattress department keep following me around like I'm going to steal something. Like I could walk out the door carrying a mattress?

I should have thought this through. I even knew about the workers permit, and I didn't plan for it. I should've known it wasn't going to work. I just ran without thinking. Stupid!

Two more laps around Macy's and I give up. I go back to Children's Place and sit on a bench outside and stare into the glass walls.

I suppose I could just sleep outside, but I've seen enough TV and heard enough stories to know what a runaway life is like. It's eating out of dumpsters, and hiding under freeways, and I'm just a kid.

I think about what going back means. And what will happen when I get there.

Can't go back there.

Plan C. Such as it is. I think I'd rather die. I have to swallow the bottle of pills this time. There is no way around it.

This is it.

I'll go back. I'll get a whipping like never before in my life. They'll yell and scream and call me all sorts of horrible names, and I'll see the hate seeping from Mom and Dad's eyes like mist. I'll wait for bedtime, take the bottle of aspirin I've been hiding in my underwear drawer to the bathroom, hide behind the shower curtain, and swallow the whole bottle, one pill at a time to keep from choking or throwing up. They'll find me in the morning when Paul gets up to take a shower before water polo practice. They'll cry at first, but then they'll be relieved.

Rose can have all my toys and clothes. I'm okay with that. Mom can sell my pawn shop violin and buy herself some new rosin, or something. That seems only fair. Paul can have my skateboard and Gwen can have back the unicorn turquoise and silver earrings.

"Hi," says a boy's voice from beside me.

Without my even noticing, the teenage cashier from Children's Place has come out into the mall and sits beside me on the bench. I feel embarrassed and caught off guard.

"Hi."

"The mall is going to close soon. You should call someone to take you home," he says.

Home?

I don't think I've had one of those in forever. But knowing the boy is right, I nod, afraid to open my mouth and speak because I'm sure a sob will creep out.

"I'd give you a ride," he says, "but I only have my driver's permit, and my mom doesn't come to pick me up for another hour."

I nod.

"Do you have any change?" he asks.

I shake my head. He digs in his pocket and hands me a couple quarters. "Here. The pay phone is right there." He points to them. It's against the wall a few yards away, in front of Macy's.

It takes me a second to swallow the lump in my throat, but I manage to say, "Thanks" without sounding too much like a baby. I get up and go to the phone.

"Good luck, gorgeous," the boy calls after me, waving and heading back into the store.

I whip around quickly, furious that he's making fun of me.

How dare he!

But, when I open my mouth to tell him to get lost I see a face in the glass walls. There's a pretty girl staring back at me. Her hair is wind tossed, wavy, and her face is full of emotion. She's got striking blue eyes behind her glasses, and is tall and slim, with a hint of curves to come. I stare at her for a split second and she stares back. I look through her to the teenage boy. He's smiling. And it's not one of those mean little wicked grins like The Creep gets whenever he's making fun of my looks, but a real smile.

Wait, I look through her?

I'm suddenly so confused I can't say anything – I just stare at the boy as he goes to his register, takes keys from his pocket and opens the cash drawer.

The girl is gone and only my reflection in the glass walls of the store looks back at me.

The girl was me. I was looking at myself and I didn't even know it.

My memory plays tricks on me. I could have sworn it was someone else. A pretty girl – a girl who looked so thoughtful, like she had a lot to say.

The boy must have felt my eyes on him because he looks up. Then the boy winks at me and smiles again, his entire face practically caving in with the deep dimples on either side of his lips.

I break eye contact because I blush. I fumble with the quarters in my hand and turn my back to the store. I face the pay phone directly in front of me on the wall.

I feel so odd I can't describe it.
Like I've seen a ghost and got kissed at the same time.

After the Jog-a-thon was the first time I'd tried to swallow the pills. There was no other way I could think to stop the pain. It wouldn't go away, no matter how hard I tried. I must be the stupidest kid on the planet. I must be the worst daughter in the world, the worst sister in the world, the worst student in the world, the worst friend in the world.

What was the use in trying?

Sitting in the bathtub, I stared at the bottle of aspirin from Mom and Dad's medicine cabinet. But then, Paul had pulled the curtain back and mentioned something about cleaning out my footprints when I got out, and I'd lost my nerve.

I needed time to prepare, so I crawled out of the bathtub and stashed the bottle under my bed.

I knew if I swallowed the whole bottle, I would go to sleep, and then I would die. I'd seen something like that from one of Gwen's soap operas. It sounded so peaceful and serene. I sat on my bed and imagined heaven to be so serene. I was sure no one in heaven would make me feel this horrible. Jesus and God would be like having a loving brother and grandpa who were nice all the time. They wouldn't tell me every time I entered the room about how imperfect I was. They'd never yell, or slap, or hurt my feelings. It sounded so lovely. And, since we weren't Catholic, I knew that killing myself wouldn't send me to hell.

I thought about the aspirin under my bed almost every day, especially on days when the picking from Gwen was more terrible than normal. I sometimes hid in my room under my bed, holding the bottle of aspirin tightly, turning it over and over in my hand, listening to the pills rolling around inside, and breathing quietly so that Gwen or Rose couldn't find me. I would lie under there and hold my breath to see if I could die that way, without taking the pills, but I always ended up gasping for air after only a few minutes. Then I would get mad at myself for being such a weakling that I couldn't even hold my breath right.

After church, every Sunday, without fail, my family had brunch at a diner. Sometimes it was Denny's or Coco's, but there was a French dip sandwich at The Silver Spoon, the diner by the Sporting Goods store and the hole in the wall Mexican restaurant, which Gwen loved and hated at the same time. Since she came back home huge and pregnant, Mom and Dad let her choose where the family had brunch, and she always chose the French Dip at The Silver Spoon, even though when it came, she'd complain and say it was soggy.

Gwen had had false labor a few times after eating there. She was pretty sure it was the horseradish sauce she put on the French dip to make it spicy.

Finally, one day, after eating the soggy French dip at The Silver Spoon, she started again. This time, though, after a few hours of counting contractions, Mom said it was time to go to the hospital. Mom and Dad went with Gwen. Louise, an old friend of Dad's from work, came and stayed at the house. Louise didn't work in computers any more, but was now studying to become a nun. She didn't wear one of those black nun dresses though, but a dark skirt, a white shirt and a grey cardigan sweater. She was a nice lady, for a nun.

Gwen had not taken any baby classes and didn't know what to expect with childbirth. Mom considered herself an expert, seen as how she had given birth to four children, but Gwen insisted that every experience was different and refused to listen to any of Mom's advice. She wouldn't get up and walk around to help the contractions, wouldn't touch the ice chips to keep from getting dehydrated, and she kept yelling at Mom to shut up.

Louise took Paul, Rose and me to the hospital a few times, while this was all happening, and Mom told Louise everything. Part of me wished I'd never overheard.

Apparently, while in the hospital they called The Creep, who was still in training in South Carolina, but he wasn't able to get leave. Instead of calming Gwen down, The Creep started yelling at her over the phone about his terrible superior officer, how he was stuck and how awful the whole thing was. When Mom saw how upset Gwen was getting, she took away the phone and The Creep cussed at Mom until she hung up. The call made Gwen's already shot nerves worse, and she panicked when she realized she would have to deliver the baby without The Creep being there.

Gwen's labor slowed once her blood pressure rose, and all attempts to help her along, including several shots of medicine from the very worried doctors, were unhelpful. An emergency cesarean was scheduled, and Gwen was whisked away to an operating room.

Gwen had a boy. She named him Christian Mitchell. Both Gwen and her son were fine. We weren't there when it happened, so Dad called the house to tell the news. Rose was so excited she opened up all the diaper packages and stacked them neatly in a row on Gwen's bed. I had a hard time being happy for Gwen. My only hope was maybe now that Gwen wasn't pregnant anymore she would be a little nicer.

A few days later The Creep came home from South Carolina but was only allowed to stay a few days. His attitude towards Mom and Dad was awful. He refused to listen to them at all. He yelled at them to mind their own business when they suggested holding up Christian's head, or burping after every ounce of formula. Gwen didn't say anything to The Creep to stop him.

Rose, Paul and I were in the waiting area at the hospital when Mom and Dad came down and told us it was time to go home. They left The Creep and Gwen at the hospital to call The Creep's dad to get a ride back to the house.

The Creep returned to South Carolina without saying anything more to Mom and Dad, and he treated me like I didn't exist, which I thought was great. He never said, "thank you" to anybody for looking after Gwen when she had his baby. But, Mom and Dad always said he was a punk.

After a few days of having the baby at home, I realized it wasn't as much fun as I had thought it would be. I kept offering to help, thinking that would smooth things over with Gwen, but it wasn't going the way I'd hoped.

"Gwen, can I hold the baby?"

"No! I just got him settled down!"

"Oh. Then can I help give him a bath tonight?"

"No! You'd probably drown him!"

"Can I heat up his bottle then?"

"Mary, go away!"

Mom and Gwen were trying to work together, changing diapers, feeding Christian and all the regular things Mom did around the house, but it never seemed to be good enough for Gwen. She was still mean, and she was still saying awful things to me all the time and for the life of me, I couldn't figure out what I was doing wrong.

The more I thought about it, the less it made sense. Maybe, I decided, it wasn't my fault, but Gwen's. Maybe Gwen was the one doing everything wrong and not me. Maybe that was why Gwen was picking on me so much, because she was just a big, fat, crazy meanie. Here Gwen had everything she had fought for after almost a year, and she was still unhappy and making everybody around her miserable. How was that my fault?

But seconds after having these thoughts, I'd remember all the other people who hated me . . . Mrs. Chastain, Jefferson Randall, Paul, Rose, Mom. Maybe even Dad. Then my emotions would flip flop from anger to sadness.

Why fight it?

I was just too stupid to understand. I finally reached the point where I didn't care about figuring it out anymore. The trouble was, I stopped caring about everything else, too.

Softball practice during Friday recess got to be a real drag. I didn't feel like running laps, or catching grounders, or doing drills for a double play. The only thing I was willing to do was hit the ball in batting practice, but most of what the team worked on was field work and we didn't get to do much hitting.

When we had practice games I had some fun, but the kids in my class were goofing off so much I got frustrated with them for wasting my time and not taking it seriously.

Grow up!

It all came tumbling down when Jefferson Randall moved second base as I was rounding first, and I got tagged out because I couldn't find where he'd moved it. All the kids in the outfield thought this was hilarious. I, on the other hand, had to be dragged away by Mrs. Mayes because I was so hopping mad. I used every cuss word I knew, kicked dirt and spat at him.

Mrs. Mayes took me to the girls' bathroom and made me rinse off my face with cold water and told me I was kicked off the team. I cried and explained what Jefferson had done, but Mrs. Mayes didn't want to hear it. She looked a little sad when she left me in the bathroom to calm down.

Things continued to get worse. When I stopped doing my extra homework for the Academic Pentathlon team, Mrs. Chastain was true to her word, and I got kicked off that too. I told Tammy and acted like I didn't care, but it was embarrassing. As far as I was concerned, this was just more proof of what a loser I was.

Oh, well.

Eventually, I got so grumpy that none of the Pretend Club wanted to play with me at recess anymore, so I went back to playing alone on the bars. The only thing I still liked was watching TV, which I seemed to be doing more and more often.

The last and final straw came when Mom yelled at me to practice my Honor Orchestra music every day, and I flat out refused. Mom screamed and hollered, grounded me from the TV for a week, took all my music and boom box away and even my skateboard, and gave me "Time Outs" in my room, forbidding me from leaving my bed, but I didn't care. I was going to swallow the bottle of aspirin eventually.

What did all this other stuff matter?

I lay on my bed, staring at the ceiling for hours and was glad for it. It was peaceful and quiet and no one bothered me, or even spoke to me, and that was what I wanted most of all. I pulled out the bottle of aspirin from under my bed and put it in my underwear drawer. It was in arms reach then, just waiting for the moment I decided I was ready. I would take it out and look at it and feel powerful. *This* I had control over. Nothing else! But *this*. Then I would put it back, because I didn't want Rose to find it and tattle on me.

Finally, Mom threatened to get the fly swatter back out and that got me to practice. Once.

I should have figured that if I didn't practice I would lose first chair in Honor Orchestra, and sure enough, that's what happened. They moved me to Second Chair and a new girl from another school sat in First. They told me I was sharing First Chair with the other girl, but I wasn't fooled. I was upset about it at first, and then I decided I didn't care about that either. At least now, I didn't have to practice every day.

Or, at least, that's what I thought. Mom had other ideas. She still kept hounding me to practice, even after I admitted to Mom what happened with first chair and the Pentathlon Team. Later, Mom took down the newspaper article and the letter from Honor Orchestra from the refrigerator, but that didn't seem to stop the nagging.

Mom persisted about practicing never giving me a moment's peace from the moment I got home from school.

Mom stood at the bottom of the stairs and yelled to the top, "The baby is awake, Mary! Practice now while you've got the chance!"

I'd yell back, "Okay." But I wouldn't stop what I was doing, which was usually nothing.

This happened every day, every twenty minutes or so.

Then, one day Mom yelled at me for the millionth time and that was when I couldn't take it anymore and I felt like my brain had exploded.

LEAVE ME ALONE!!!

I took out my bottle of aspirin and stared at it for a long time. I thought and thought about it. I even opened the child-proof cap and placed the bottle to my lips. But then I put the bottle down; I couldn't bring myself to do it. Something was stopping me and I had no idea what it was. Finally, frustrated that I was such a chicken, I put the bottle back into the drawer and walked out the front door when no one was looking.

It would be better to run away and be by herself living in the mall than to be dead, or worse yet, in that house with those people for one more minute. For a single solitary minute!

Done, I tell you. Done!

And that brought me past the houses, and Tammy's, past the old perfect house, and the school, past the park and the diner, to the mall.

10

MARY

I stand in front of the pay phone for a few minutes, the quarters in my hand. What just happened? The boy called me gorgeous. But, I'm not. I'm stupid, ugly, useless nobody Mary. Doesn't he see that? Wasn't it obvious?

The girl in the glass had been gorgeous, but that hadn't been me.

I mean, it was, but that's not how I really am. Is it?

I snap out of my haze enough to use the phone. But, before I push the coins into the slot I get tapped on the shoulder.

It's Mr. and Mrs. Burns. They're from church and close friends with Reverend McCormack. I must look terrible because they stare at me hard.

"Mary? Is everything all right?" Mrs. Burns asks.

Even though I'm hungry and thirsty and cold and tired and humiliated, I say, "Yes."

"What are you doing here this late? Are you by yourself?" Mr. Burns asks.

I point to the phone. "I was just about to call for a ride."

"Did you come here all by yourself?" Mrs. Burns asks.

I sigh and nod, feeling my throat go tight again.

Here it comes.

I'm going to get a lecture on worrying my family sick and how dumb I am for running away to the mall when I'm too young to get a job.

Idiot.

I look to the floor and feel my shoulders hang as I wait for the yelling to start.

Mr. Burns raises his hand to run it through his hair, and I can't help it, but I flinch.

To my complete shock, Mrs. Burns starts to get all watery in the eyes and Mr. Burns sighs so loudly, I take a step back. Mrs. Burns comes around me and puts her arm around my shoulder like I'm made of glass or something and squeezes me softly into her side. "Come on, honey," she said. "We're friends of Reverend McCormack. We have an idea of what's happening at home, and we want to help."

They do?

I swallow hard and think that if they only knew half of it, they wouldn't be helping me home.

Mr. Burns takes a cell phone from his pocket and asks me the number. After someone answers at the house, Mrs. Burns leads me away from him and into the middle of the mall. I look over at Children's Place, and through the glass, the boy watches. I half grin at him, and he waves back. He probably thinks Mr. and Mrs. Burns are my folks, which is okay by me.

Mr. and Mrs. Burns drive me home. On the way, they both ask if there is anything I would like to tell them and invite me to free counseling sessions with Reverend McCormack. Even though they're nice and look really worried and probably will listen to me, I remember Mom's speech about family loyalty, and how Mrs. Chastain didn't believe me, so I figure there is no point in telling. I tell them everything is fine and, "No thanks." It's nice of them to ask, though.

When they pull in front of my house, I get out and wave them off. I don't want them to see me getting yelled at.

"Are you sure you're all right?" Mr. Burns asks again. I nod. "Yeah."

Mrs. Burns frowns. She looks upset and I feel bad for

her. I don't mean to make her sad, and I'm not sure how I've done it.

Inside, Mom, Dad, Paul, Gwen and Rose are in the family room. Christian is in his bassinette, in the corner. I see his arms flail. Mom hangs up everybody's winter coats in the hall closet, and Dad's holding a flashlight in each hand looking as purple as a plum. My best guess is that they were headed outside to try and look for me when Mr. Burns called. I know I should feel guilty about that, but instead I'm glad.

Serves them right!

I'm thrilled they were worried! I hope I ruined their dinner!

Gwen is the first to speak, which doesn't surprise me. "You've got a lot of nerve," she says.

Dad shoots Gwen a nasty look and to my amazement, she shuts up.

"Feel better now?" Dad says. He sounds completely ticked off.

"Yes!" I say, as rudely as I can. I have nothing to lose now. It's better to get the slap over and done with. I brace for the impact but nothing comes.

Mom slams the closet door shut after hanging the coats, takes the flashlights from Dad, and walks out of the family room. She hasn't even looked at me since my return.

"Mom and Dad were worried sick," Gwen snaps.

From behind Gwen, Paul laughs. Everyone turns and

looks at him. It's a good ten seconds of him laughing before he raises his hands in the air, as if to say, "I give up."

"That's hysterical, coming from you." Gwen hisses at him like a snake.

Paul rolls his eyes and follows Mom out of the family room and grabs Rose by the arm as he leaves, taking her with him. On his way out, he raises his eyebrows to signal he's not mad at me.

Dad glares at me and frowns deeply. He looks like he's got a lot to say, but instead he says, "We're going to dinner." Dad traipses down the hall to the garage and the car.

I stand alone in the family room. Is that it? No lecture? No whipping?

I get in the car with everybody else and nobody says a word.

Not a peep.

We go to dinner at a fast food restaurant, but I'm not hungry. I keep looking at my father, waiting for his face to stop being purple. But it stays that color for the rest of the night.

Later that night, before bed, I rummage in my underwear drawer and pull out the bottle of aspirin. Rose is in the top bunk, pretending to be asleep.

I stand in the darkness, holding the bottle.

I think about the boy and his wink. I wonder what his name is.

I think about my family, and what they will be like after I use the bottle of aspirin. I remember my father's purple face at the fast food restaurant and the image reminds me of another time he looked that awful.

Gwen's wedding.

I'm suddenly filled with guilt.

Can you imagine how he'd look if I died?

It would crush him. He wouldn't be purple, he'd be a color yet to be discovered. And it would be all my fault. After everything Gwen has done to my family, what I've planned is worse. I see that.

It's inexcusable, and selfish, cruel.

I cry, quietly, so's not to wake Rose from her pretend sleep.

My plans are worse than Gwen's meanness, and her lashing out. It's the ultimate in hate.

I don't hate my family. I don't. The last thing I want to do is hurt them, no matter what else has happened. I never thought about that.

The bottle feels heavy.

I pad down the hall to the bathroom and place the bottle of aspirin back into the medicine cabinet, snapping it closed.

I stare at the girl in the mirror, but it's just me.

My hair is a mess, and my eyes are a bit swollen from all the crying today. My teeth are still crooked and my nose is too round.

The girl in the glass looks nothing like who I really am. Yet, we're the same person. How can that be?

I think I will try to be more like her. The girl in the glass looked very mature and wise. Like she *knew* things.

I go back to bed.

It takes me a while to fall asleep.

11

MARY

The next morning is a Saturday, so the entire family hangs out together. Leaving Gwen and the baby at home, Mom, Dad, Rose and I go to Paul's water polo match in the morning, and then come home for lunch. Nobody talks about what happened the day before. Nobody says much of anything. I try not to sound stupid and figure I'll escape any further punishment if I keep quiet.

I watch every word I say. I avoid Gwen like the plague. It seems to be working.

At the end of lunch, Mom asks me to clear the dishes,

and while doing so I accidentally drop a plate. It chips, but doesn't break because I slam my knee up against it and trap it on the kitchen cabinet under the sink so it doesn't hit the floor.

The commotion wakes poor sleeping Christian in his bassinette in the family room. Gwen gets mad and screams at me. Again.

"You dummy!" she yells.

"Sorry."

Mom comes over and helps me clean up the kitchen cabinet. She feels the chip on the plate and figures it isn't sharp enough to hurt anybody and puts it in the sink with the other dirty dishes. I turn on the water to scrub them as Gwen gets Christian to calm down. She sits down at the kitchen table, glaring at me.

"Seriously, Mary, what is wrong with you?" she says.

I'm not sure how I'm supposed to answer, but it turns out I don't need to because Mom beats me to it.

"Leave her alone!" she hisses.

I feel the earth shift on its axis. Have I just heard that right? I stare at Mom. It's the only time, ever, I've heard someone defend me against Gwen. Ever! I'm at the sink with the water running, my mouth open.

Gwen goes straight to screaming. "Mom!"

Mom turns to face Gwen and leans her palms on the

kitchen table. "You have done nothing but pick on Mary since the moment you got back. Enough!"

"She woke up Christian!" Gwen shouts, causing the baby to stir and cry in his bassinette.

"Her life is a living hell because of you, and I'm telling you to knock . . . it . . . off!"

Gwen ignores Mom's last statement and picks up the baby.

I can't look away from Mom. When our eyes meet, I see a look I've never seen before. Mom's mouth is set, but not frowning; her eyes are hard, but not harsh. Mom reaches over and pats me on the shoulder. I can't believe it. Then Mom's eyes look at me like she knows everything. Like she knows what it's like to do everything wrong, to have a mom who loses it and hits you, to have a sister who won't stop picking on you. Mom looks at me like we are the same.

"Mary," Mom says, "go upstairs."

I can't escape fast enough. In fact, I forget to shut off the running water and Mom has to reach over and do it for me as I sprint up the stairs. I plop onto the top step and lean forward so I can listen. Paul's bedroom door opens and he sits as well. He's obviously heard Mom yelling at Gwen. I dare not look at him.

"Dennis!" Mom shouts. "Get in here, it's time." I hear the back sliding glass door open and shut. "Gwen, we need to talk to you," Mom says.

"Yeah? What about?" Gwen's attitude is still dripping from her every word.

"We've purchased you a ticket to South Carolina. You leave tonight. We'll ship your things to you later." Dad is talking now.

"What?" Gwen must have been holding Christian, because I hear him grunt when she shouts. "I can't go there! There isn't any family housing!"

"I spoke with the commanding officer this morning. There are some off-base apartments where a lot of families live. We'll help with the rent. It's all arranged," Dad says.

"You talked with who?" Gwen is still shouting, but I notice Mom and Dad sound calm.

"You can't stay here anymore," Dad says.

"It's time you were on your own," Mom adds. "You wanted to get married, you wanted to raise the baby; now, you need to start your life as a grown up, and you can't do it here."

"You're kicking me out?" Gwen sounds like she's about to cry. I actually feel bad for her.

"It's for the best," Mom says.

"But . . . but . . ." Gwen is at a loss for words, which, I'm sure, has never happened before. "The baby . . . he's too young."

"He'll sleep through the flight," Mom says. "I've packed your diaper bag with everything you'll need."

"You went through my diaper bag?" Gwen screams. Mom and Dad ignore the bait and keep on track.

"After you get there, you're on your own," Dad says. "I suggest you have . . . " He pauses for a second, "your *husband*," now I can hear Dad's sarcasm, "meet you at the airport with a baby seat."

"You can't do this!" Gwen shouts, causing Christian to grunt again.

"We can and we are," Dad says.

"But . . . why? I don't understand! You're kicking out your own grandchild?" Gwen is so furious her voice shakes.

"No, Gwen." Mom says, "We're giving you what you've always wanted. We're treating you like an adult."

"This is bull . . . !" Gwen shouts. She proceeds to curse and yell at our parents for a few minutes. Mom and Dad don't say anything until she pauses for breath. ". . . completely out of the blue . . . " Gwen's saying, ". . . and for no good reason whatsoever!"

Someone slams his or her hand against the kitchen table because there's a loud boom. The baby wails. I guess it's Dad because he's the next to speak, shouting above the baby's screams. "Our reasons are completely valid and a long time coming! You are a negative person, Gwen!"

"Dennis," Mom says, as if she's warning him.

"You have been unhappy here and making everybody else

unhappy right along with you," Dad says. "You don't want to be here, so just go. We'll all get along a lot better the moment you do."

"I hate you!" Gwen screams, and Christian bellows along with her. "I'll never forgive you for this!"

"We're doing you a favor!" Dad hollers. "We're helping to pay for your apartment! A little gratitude from you would not be out of line!"

Gwen scoffs. "Gratitude for kicking me out? Whatever!"

Someone breezes past the stairwell and a door slams. Then it gets quiet.

Paul gets up and is about to walk away when we hear hushed voices in the kitchen. He quickly sits back down and leans over farther.

"You alright?" Mom asks.

"Ask me again in twenty years," Dad replies.

"Think it'll help?" Mom says.

"We'll see. The counselor says it's the first step to getting them back on track. I never realized how bad it was until she was gone and then came back. You know, between the two of you, it's a miracle she didn't run away sooner," Dad says.

Paul looks at me, but I can't meet his gaze. I stare at the carpet and listen.

"I'm not going to mess up the rest like I did Gwen," Dad

adds. "I'm *not* doing it again. We've got to do better, Betty. And *you've* got to stop! This hasn't been working."

There's a pause and Mom sighs. "I know."

Paul stands from the step and goes back to his room. He turns on heavy metal and I figure he's fine.

Back in my room, I feel strange. I sit on my bottom bunk and stare at the floor for a minute. Rose has set up the Barbie house and plays on the floor. There's little tables and chairs and bottle caps that we use for plates all in the wrong places. I consider fixing them for Rose, but change my mind.

"I can't get the table to stop falling over," Rose sighs, upset.

I watch my baby sister and feel sorry for her. She doesn't have any idea what's about to happen. This time, though, I feel responsible for Rose. After all, I'm the big sister now.

"Here," I say, moving across the room to help her. "Let me try."

Gwen leaves after Rose and I go to bed. When she isn't at breakfast, the only one who asks where she's gone is Rose. Rose is very sad, and cries in Mom's lap for a few minutes after they tell her that Gwen and the baby have moved away. Mom cries, too.

Weeks pass and we don't hear from Gwen. Mom and Dad are worried, but try not to show it. Every time the phone rings, they practically jump from their seats to race to get it. It's never Gwen, though.

ANNE TIBBETS

After the fog of bad feelings begins to lift, we get back to normal things. The whole family, or, what's left of it, come to my Honor Orchestra concert and gives me flowers afterwards, and Dad comes to the softball game at the end of the school year and sits with me in the stands, even though I'm not playing anymore.

At one point while the teams are switching offense and defense, he bumps me with his shoulder.

"How you doing, Mary?"

"Fine." I watch Jenny Savage take my old position at second base and get an ice bucket feeling in my stomach.

"No," Dad says, and he sounds serious this time. "How are you doing?" He looks at my face like he's searching for crumbs I've forgotten to wipe off.

"I'm okay."

Dad puts his lips together. "Better now?"

I can't look at his face. "Yeah."

"Even so, Mom and I want you to talk to somebody. She's a member of the church and a counselor. We think it would be good for you." He looks like he's in pain. "We know it was rough. . . ."

I know Dad's trying to be nice but I don't want to talk about it anymore. I don't want to think about what it was like, or how I felt. Maybe someday I will, but not yet. Despite these feelings, my desire to please him is stronger. "Okay, Dad."

He opens his mouth to say something else, but I cut him off. "I'm okay, Dad."

He watches the players on the field. "You promise?"

My feet dangle on the bleachers and I grip the metal with my hands on either side of my legs. "I promise."

Dad claps because one of the sixth graders catches a grounder. I don't clap along. I don't feel like it. I feel guilty for what I almost did. Besides, Dad doesn't realize he's clapping for Jefferson Randall.

A month later school ends, and summer comes. The first few weeks I don't do anything, but Mom sees an ad in the paper for a babysitting class at the hospital and makes me sign up. I take the class and tell people at church I'm "certified," and funny enough, I get a few regular clients. I spend all my babysitting money on new books, and do a lot of reading.

I give all my Barbie things to Rose and tell her she can keep them. I try hard not to correct Rose when she sets up the house wrong. I play at Tammy's and eat all the cardboard cookies her mother offers. I talk to the counselor at church once a week. I'm not sure it's making any difference, but it makes my parents happy, so I don't complain. Though, I have to admit it isn't quite as painful to talk about Gwen as it was in the beginning. I'm almost ready to tell her about the bottle of aspirin.

The house gets quiet and calm, and for a while it seems

fake. As the summer passes, we get used to it and then it seems normal to be in a house without screaming again. In fact, we all get along fine. We're more careful of the quiet the second time around, knowing that at any moment, we can hear from Gwen and the calm will shatter.

Near the end of the summer I almost feel happy. I remember the girl in the glass and I think I'm more like her, and don't feel like such a loser. Plus, it helps that I'm not hearing about it all the time. But I don't trust compliments either. They will forever seem insincere to me. The clouds lift, yet still, to me there are always dried raindrop spots on the windows that never wash off.

After his fifteenth birthday, Paul gets a job in the mall at the frozen yogurt shop. When we visit him at work to get some yogurt, I sometimes see the boy from Children's Place. He acts like he doesn't know me at all, so I figure he's forgotten about me. Or, maybe he doesn't know who I am without my face being red from crying.

Almost a year after that first conversation in Gwen's room, it's my thirteenth birthday. Mom and Dad get me contact lenses so I don't have to wear glasses anymore. I also grow several inches and have to start buying new clothes in the junior department, instead of the girls'. I've grown out my hair, too; it touches my shoulders and has gotten really wavy.

To my surprise, I'm not half bad looking without two giant

coke-bottle lenses in front of my face, and clothes that don't look like they belong in another decade. Soon after that, one of the boys in our church youth group asks me if I want to go to a movie with him.

Mom and Dad don't seem too shocked when I ask them if I can go.

"Sure," Dad says. He grins like he's thinking of something funny. "But, only a matinee, and it can't be an R-rated movie."

"And come home right afterwards," Mom adds.

"Which boy is this? The blond one or the dark haired one?" Dad asks.

"The dark one. His name is Charlie Ruthford."

"I thought I saw him eyeing you," Dad says, poking me in the ribs with his finger.

"No way!" I giggle. "Really?"

"Why wouldn't he, Mary?" Mom says. "You're such a smart and pretty girl."

I blush about eight hundred different colors of red as my eyes catch the sunlight shining clearly through the kitchen window. For the first time, I know it's the truth.

ACKNOWLEDGMENTS

I want to extend a warm and hearty thank you to Premier Digital Publishing, my agent Joel Gotler, Kib Prestridge for the incredible cover which literally took my breath away, and to my editor Noelle McDonald, for their parts in making *Shut Up* possible.

I also want to acknowledge my family. My husband Daniel, and my girls, who put up with me during the tumultuous three years it took me to write this novel. My family soldiered my process with honor and understanding. Thank you!

Part of that writing process is to listen to music that inspires the mood and emotional struggles of the characters. If you, the reader, are interested in hearing the musical inspiration for *Shut Up*, find the song "Simon," by Lifehouse. It still gives me chills and brings me to tears nearly every time.

Shut Up is extremely personal to me. Parts of this book are based on actual events from my childhood. Some of these events I left exactly as they happened; like the teacher's response to Mary's crying in class. That was taken verbatim from my memory. But in the course of the eight drafts that existed of this novel, other memories from my youth were grossly distorted, warped, exaggerated, and completely fictionalized in order to make *Shut Up* stronger. This is particularly true when it comes to Mary's family.

This is not a memoir. This is fiction.

Please keep that in mind should you know my family. They have to put up with me, and they are enduring the publication of this book – they don't need any further grief. Many of them have opted not to read it at all. I fully support this decision.

Please respect that.

Many Thanks,
Anne

OPEN ROAD
INTEGRATED MEDIA

Open Road Integrated Media is a digital publisher and multimedia content company. Open Road creates connections between authors and their audiences by marketing its ebooks through a new proprietary online platform, which uses premium video content and social media.